Praise for

Princess of Glass

"*Princess of Glass* does Cinderella proud." —*Chicago YA Fiction Examiner*

"In a clever reworking of the Cinderella story, George once again proves adept at spinning her own magical tale. Fans of Donna Jo Napoli's retellings will cheer loudly as George proves her own mettle." —*Booklist*

"George delivers another satisfying fairy-tale retelling. . . . Poppy is intrepid and forthright, refreshing qualities in a fairy-tale princess. Christian is an affable hero who is far from perfect—and sometimes quite helpless (also a refreshing change, for a fairy-tale prince). . . . As with George's other retellings, be prepared for plenty of twists." —*VOYA*

Praise for

Princess of the Midnight Ball

"This is a well-realized and fast-paced fantasy-romance that will find favor among fans of fairy tales, feisty heroines, and dashing young men with strength, cunning, and sensitivity." —*Booklist*

"Fans of fairy-tale retellings like Robin McKinley's *Beauty* or Gail Carson Levine's *Ella Enchanted* will enjoy this story for its magic, humor, and touch of romance." —*SLJ*

Books by Jessica Day George

Dragon Slippers
Dragon Flight
Dragon Spear

~

Sun and Moon, Ice and Snow

~

Princess of the Midnight Ball
Princess of Glass

~

Tuesdays at the Castle

Princess of Glass

Jessica Day George

NEW YORK BERLIN LONDON SYDNEY

For my own Princess,
who danced before she could crawl

First published in the United States of America in June 2010
by Bloomsbury Books for Young Readers
Paperback edition published in June 2011
www.bloomsburyteens.com

For information about permission to reproduce selections from this book, write to Permissions, Bloomsbury BFYR, 175 Fifth Avenue, New York, New York 10010

The Library of Congress has cataloged the hardcover edition as follows:
George, Jessica Day.
Princess of glass/by Jessica Day George. —1st U.S. ed.
p. cm.
Summary: In the midst of maneuverings to create political alliances through marriage, sixteen-year-old Poppy, one of the infamous twelve dancing princesses, becomes the target of a vengeful witch while Prince Christian ties to save her.
ISBN 978-1-59990-478-8 (hardcover)
[1. Fairy tales. 2. Princesses—Fiction. 3. Princes—Fiction. 4. Witches—Fiction. 5. Magic—Fiction.] I. Twelve dancing princesses. English II. Title.
PZ8.G3295Prc 2010 [Fic]—dc22 2009046895

ISBN 978-1-59990-659-1 (paperback)

Book design by Donna Mark
Typeset by Westchester Book Composition
Printed in the U.S.A. by Quad/Graphics, Fairfield, Pennsylvania
1 3 5 7 9 10 8 6 4 2

All papers used by Bloomsbury Publishing, Inc., are natural, recyclable products made from wood grown in well-managed forests. The manufacturing processes conform to the environmental regulations of the country of origin.

Prologue

"Perfect," the Corley said, lips stretched wide in a smile. She took a shallow pan of molten glass and set it in the air over her head. "Yes, everything will be perfect this time."

She tilted the pan just a little, and the syrupy stuff slithered out in a green sheet. It flowed, pale and smooth, into a basin, and showed the Corley a young girl with blue eyes and black hair under a little white cap. She was ironing a muslin gown, a grim expression on her face.

"She is beautiful," pronounced the witch. "And clever. But almost . . . obsessed with her loss. Perfect. She will come to me with open arms, the lovely. And now for her prince."

She tipped the pan a little, pouring out more liquid glass, and there he was. A tall youth with pale gold hair and deep blue eyes, riding a showy gray horse down a city street. All around him, women stopped to sigh but he rode on, oblivious.

"Handsome, yet blind to his own appeal and so much more," the Corley purred. "And it was so easy to bring him here."

The thick green liquid flickered and another face appeared. Black hair framed a face with porcelain skin and large violet eyes. The young girl's beauty was only marred by the frown she wore.

Curious, the Corley watched as the frowning girl was kissed and hugged by a whole herd of other young ladies, clearly all sisters. Last of all two tall young men embraced her. One of the young men handed over a bag that appeared to be full of balls of yarn with a pair of sharp knitting needles sticking out of the top. The girl finally laughed, and the other young man helped her into a carriage.

"What's this, what's this?" The Corley clucked her tongue when the steam failed to show her any more. "Another one coming? Ah, me! Can nothing I seek come easily?

"Still, what's one more little girl?"

Houseguest

When someone knocked on the bedroom door, Poppy nearly leaped right off the bed. She had been sprawled across it writing, and her quill pen skidded over the paper and left huge blotches of ink on the letter to her twin, Daisy.

"Oh, blast!" Poppy dabbed at the ink with her handkerchief before it could run off the paper and onto the white counterpane. "Yes? Come in."

After sharing a room with her twin and their sister Orchid all her life, Poppy was not used to people knocking on her bedroom door. Nor was the silence of Seadown House at all soothing, but only seemed to magnify the least squeak or whisper, until Poppy thought her nerves would never settle.

Lady Margaret peeped around the doorframe. She had been the greatest beauty of her generation, and her looks had not faded with age. Her hair gleamed like polished wood and her large brown eyes sparkled. She smiled kindly at Poppy, who was still dabbing at the letter with her ruined handkerchief.

"I hope I didn't startle you, my dear."

Years ago Poppy would have said yes and indignantly displayed the ruined letter. But Rose and Lily, her oldest sisters, had been teaching her tact with great determination, and so she shook her head.

"Not at all," she replied. "I've made a muddle of this letter without any help."

Lady Margaret came all the way into the room. She took the pen and ink from Poppy and set it on the writing desk without comment. Poppy felt a pang: she *should* sit at the desk to compose her letters, but it was so hard to break the habit of lounging while she wrote.

Lady Margaret turned the elegant little desk chair to face the bed and sat down. "Marianne tells me that you don't wish to attend the Thwaites' ball," she said, her voice beautifully modulated as always.

Poppy reflected that it was no wonder she had been shipped off to Breton. Lady Margaret Seadown, Poppy's late mother's cousin, was all that was elegant and refined. Poppy suspected that her father, King Gregor, was hoping for some of Lady Margaret's elegance to rub off on her.

Fighting down her feeling of panic at the very mention of a ball, Poppy took command of her own voice and said merely, "I'm sorry, Cousin Margaret, but I don't dance."

Lady Margaret's brow furrowed delicately. "But my dear, the unpleasantness with the dancing slippers . . ." She let the question trail away.

Poppy winced, clenching her fist around the ink-stained

handkerchief. Yes, the "unpleasantness" with the dancing slippers.

From the time she could walk until she was thirteen years old, Poppy had spent nearly every night dancing. Dancing until her toes bled and her satin slippers were worn to shreds, and her eleven sisters with her. Until Galen, now married to her oldest sister, Rose, had rescued them from the curse that had begun with their mother's foolish bargain nineteen years before.

"I *can* dance," Poppy clarified. "But I really prefer not to." *Ever again*, she added silently. Rose and Galen sometimes danced together, out in the garden with a little impromptu music courtesy of her sister Violet. But the royal family of Westfalin had neither hosted nor attended a ball in three years, though they had banquets and concerts and parties enough to befit their status.

"I see," Lady Margaret said.

But it was clear that she didn't. No one did. And as fond as Poppy was of her mother's elegant cousin, she could not enlighten her.

By the time Galen had helped free her family, the Church was investigating Poppy and her sisters on charges of witchcraft, and nine princes were dead. Their only crime had been trying to solve the mystery and perhaps win a royal bride, but the King Under Stone, the horrible creature with whom Poppy's mother had made her bargain, had killed them all. Since then they had all agreed—King Gregor, the sisters, and Galen—that none of them would speak of the curse or the King Under Stone again.

"But my dear," Lady Margaret went on. "Please consider attending the ball even if you don't dance. The Thwaites are charming, and their social occasions are the height of fashion. There will be wonderful music, and food, and so many fine young people for you to meet. And I hate to have you languishing at home alone while we enjoy ourselves." She made a face. "I would stay home with you, but Marianne will be heartbroken if she cannot attend, and I must chaperone her."

Poppy had to think about it for a while.

A long while.

She was not given to fearful turns or attacks of the vapors like some girls (including several of her sisters). But most of her life had been a nightmare of endless, sleepless nights dancing in the arms of the half-mortal son of a half-mortal king. She had no happy memories of balls.

But she would not let old fear rule her life, she decided. During the three weeks that she had been in Breton, the Seadowns had been invited to no less than seven balls, and turned them all down because they did not want their guest to feel abandoned. She could not in good conscience ask them to give up another invitation just because she was feeling missish. She was fairly certain that the Thwaites were not evil incarnate, and they would not try to kidnap her. She would go, and she would enjoy herself.

Even if she could not bring herself to dance.

Poppy realized she had been holding her breath and let it out now in a whoosh. "I'll go," she said to Lady Margaret. "Thank you for understanding if I don't dance, however."

"Of course, my dear." Lady Margaret smiled radiantly and patted Poppy's hand. "I'll tell Marianne and Richard. We'll have a cold supper, and then Gabrielle will help you dress."

She glided from the room, and Poppy set aside her ruined handkerchief and letter. She would write to Daisy later. For now she opened her wardrobe and brought out two gowns from the very back. Her oldest sister, Rose, had had them made for her.

"You'll need ball gowns," Rose had insisted.

"I'm not going to any balls," Poppy objected.

"You might surprise yourself," Galen had said. "You'll have friends; you'll want to go to a ball with them . . ." He had raised his eyebrows suggestively as he knit away with two tiny wooden needles and yarn that was hardly thicker than a thread.

"No."

But Rose had had the maids pack the two gowns behind Poppy's back. And Poppy would never let Rose know that she was suddenly grateful for the gowns. In fact, Poppy debated whether she would even tell her own twin that she had been to a ball. Daisy practically had hysterics when their sister Violet played a *valse* on the pianoforte.

Young Bretoner ladies wore white to most formal occasions, which made Poppy feel like a corpse. Clever Rose, knowing this, had had these gowns made of fine white muslin with satin slips of a different color underneath. One slip was purple, which the white muslin softened to lavender, the other a rich blue dampened into a mistier shade by the overgown. There was delicate embroidery around the hems and necklines to match

the underskirts. Poppy laid the lavender gown across the bed (after checking to make certain that she had not spilled any ink on the counterpane) and then went downstairs. Suddenly hungry, she wanted to find out how soon the early supper would be.

Prince

Prince Christian rode with his eyes focused straight ahead. As long as he didn't make eye contact with any of the girls lining the streets of Damerhavn to watch him go by, they wouldn't do anything foolish.

Like pretend to faint under the hooves of his horse.

Or throw a handkerchief at him, hoping that he would keep it as a memento.

The last time that had happened, his horse had spooked at the sight of the white fluttery thing, and Christian had nearly been thrown into the waiting arms of a horde of hopeful young ladies. He wanted to ride, needed to get out of the palace and away from his parents and tutors, but it was never as relaxing as he hoped it would be.

Today he was even more distracted than usual. On his way to the stables, his father had popped out of his study and made Christian promise to speak with him immediately upon his return.

Christian had extended his daily ride to stall for time.

With a sigh, he saw from the angle of the sun that if he didn't return to the palace soon his father would send soldiers to find him. Not because he was a prisoner, but because Christian's parents loved him, and cared for him, and worried for his safety.

Constantly.

"You're alive today because we smother you," King Karl was fond of saying when Christian accused his parents of being overprotective. "Imagine if we'd sent you off to Westfalin, and you'd had your soul sucked away by those horrible girls!"

Mention of this always made Christian uncomfortable. When the king of Westfalin had pleaded for a prince to help solve the mystery behind the princesses' worn-out dancing shoes, Christian had been eager to go. His parents, however, had not permitted it. From the beginning they had been certain that dark magic was involved, and when the reports came of the failed princes dying in strange accidents, King Karl had put Christian under house arrest. No son of his would sneak away to Westfalin and attempt to meddle with those "cursed girls."

Not that Christian had wanted to get married. He had only been fifteen at the time, after all. But he had never been outside of the Danelaw, and it all sounded like such a great adventure. In the end it had been a common soldier who had solved the mystery and ended up being knighted and married to the oldest princess. The intrepid fellow had solved the problem using an embroidery hoop or some such strange thing, but Christian rather doubted that part of the story.

Back at the palace, Christian groomed his horse himself,

still trying to put off this talk. Then he had to go and change out of his riding clothes, wash his face, and comb his hair—which needed to be cut, he noticed—and find his father. The king was not in his study after all, but up on the roof of the palace where a telescope had been mounted next to the pole bearing the royal flag.

"See this?" King Karl pointed the telescope at the harbor and gestured for Christian to look through it.

He looked. "It's the harbor," he said.

"I know it's the harbor, Christian," his father said patiently. "Look at the ships in it."

"Two of our navy gunners and a merchant from Norskland," Christian reported, not sure where his father was going with all this.

"And there, to the left of the Norske ship?"

"It looks like a Bretoner." Christian pulled away from the eyepiece to blink for a moment, then looked again. "Yes, a Bretoner galley. Royal Navy, in fact."

"Very good." King Karl nodded in approval. "Yesterday I received the ambassador from Breton. It seems that King Rupert has some ideas about the future of Ionia." Karl chuckled. "Funny, isn't it? When Breton is doing well, they're an island unto themselves, but if there's ever any unrest, suddenly 'all the nations of Ionia need to band together.' "

Not knowing how to reply to this, Christian merely continued to look at the harbor through the telescope. A sinking feeling was growing in his stomach, however, and he knew that somehow this news from Breton involved him.

"Westfalin's war with Analousia was not a pretty thing," King Karl went on. "It cost a lot of lives, and caused a lot of bad blood between former allies. Then there was that business with Gregor's gaggle of daughters and those fool princes dying left and right."

The Westfalian princesses again. The back of Christian's neck prickled.

"A lot of old alliances need renewing," his father was saying. "Rupert's quite concerned about it, and I know that Francesco of Spania's been talking about the same thing for a while. Some official state visits and exchanging of gifts would not be remiss."

"Do you want me to send a gift to Prince George?" Christian had met the heir to the Bretoner throne once before, and he was a nice enough chap if a bit too obsessed with foxhunting. Christian shrugged. "I could send him a new riding crop or some such."

But his father was shaking his head. "Well." King Karl paused. "I suppose if you wanted to take a gift to George you could. But that's not exactly what we have in mind."

Christian's heart began to race. "*Take* a gift? You want me to go to *Breton*?" Christian blurted out the question, incredulous.

King Karl nodded, looking uncomfortable.

Jaw agape, Christian stared at his father. He'd been to Breton once, as a child, and once to Analousia before the war, but since then he'd had to fight to even leave the palace grounds. Now his father wanted to send him to Breton?

"Why? Why now?"

"Because we must," King Karl said simply. "As I said, since the war, things haven't been right between the nations of Ionia, and the Westfalian princesses did nothing to improve that. It's time to prove to our neighbors that we trust one another—"

Christian interrupted. "Do we?"

His father looked grim. "We pretend that we do," he said. "And we pretend that we aren't all thinking the same thing: that the death of so many princes has left a lot of countries in a vulnerable state. Not all of those poor boys were second sons, you know. Helvetia sent their only heir, the next in line is a cousin's son. Unless Markus decides to take Westfalin's lead and declare his daughter and her future husband co-rulers."

Frowning, Christian asked, "Who is she going to marry?" His tutors had drilled the names of every royal family in Ionia into his head, but it always seemed that there were so many young princesses that their names blurred together in his mind.

"No one yet, and that's what makes Rupert's little plan so perfect. We're going to be exchanging our sons and daughters for a while: sending you to Breton while George goes to Analousia, and Analousia's little Prince Henri comes here. Ostensibly it's to make friends among the next generation, but go a little deeper and it's a grand matchmaking scheme."

"What?"

"That's right," King Karl laughed. "Think about it: George will leave for Analousia shortly after you arrive in Breton, and then you'll be at the mercy of his sisters and cousins. You'll come back here for the holidays with your family; your mother

put her foot down over that. But after the New Year I might have you visit Spania, or La Belge, we've just sent them a courier. There are a number of lovely ladies at those courts as well, and you, my boy, are of an age when you should be thinking of a royal alliance."

Christian felt as though his world were dropping out from under him. In the space of a few hours he had gone from feeling smothered by his parents to being thrown to the wolves, so to speak. He would be alone in a strange country, expected to talk and flirt and possibly even marry some silly princess.

And if he failed, another war might break out.

This wasn't remotely what he had thought his father wanted to talk about. Christian slapped the side of the telescope and watched it spin on its tripod. He was being offered an adventure, but was it one he wanted to embark on? There would be no battles to fight on horseback and with rifle in hand, only fancy dress parties and balls.

King Karl's gaze softened and he put one hand on the young man's shoulder. "Son, we need you to do this. You know your mother and I have always tried to keep you safe," his voice roughened and he barked a laugh. "All right, we've fussed like a hen with a new chick. But it's because you're our only son and we love you. Sending one's heir off to a foreign land is never an easy thing, but your sisters are too young. Your mother and I, well, we paced the floor all night arguing about what to do. And we think that this is the right thing." Karl looked down for a moment. "If you cannot bring yourself to go, we'll make other arrangements." The king grimaced.

It was reassuring to know that this wasn't an easy decision for his parents. For a brief, wild moment Christian had been wondering if they wanted to be rid of him after all.

But at last he was being offered a chance to travel! Even if it wasn't where or how he had dreamed, it was better than nothing.

"I'll go," Christian said.

His father gave him a rough, quick hug. "Good lad."

Ball

Poppy regretted her decision to go to the ball as soon as they entered the Thwaites' mansion. The dancing had already started and music poured down the stairs, making Marianne clutch at Poppy's arm in excitement. The Thwaites were standing at the top of the stairs to receive their guests, and they were delighted to see Poppy, the mysterious foreign princess.

"Oh, Your Highness," Lady Thwaite gushed. "We're honored to have you join us! I'm sure your dance card will be filled before you have time to sit down."

Wishing that she could sink into the floor as the guests gathered in the foyer turned to gawk at her, Poppy just nodded and smiled. Then Marianne burst out with the news that Poppy didn't dance, and they spent ten minutes explaining that she was not ill, and she really did want to attend the ball, and thanking their gracious hosts, until Poppy felt like she was baring her teeth in self-defense rather than smiling.

It started all over again when they stepped into the ballroom. A footman bustled over to hand the ladies their dance cards, and was confused when Lady Margaret took one, Marianne took one, but Poppy did not. They found some seats along one wall near some friends of the Seadowns' and young men started coming over to sign their cards. Again Poppy had to decline any dances, holding up her left hand to show that she had no dance card dangling from her gloved wrist.

"But surely you'll make an exception for me," said one duke's son, lowering his eyelids in a flirtatious manner.

"Is there something in your eye?" Poppy tried to assume a solicitous expression.

"Er, no." The duke's son backed away, and Poppy fought back a pang of guilt.

It was all very well, she thought to herself, to say that choosing not to dance at a ball will be no great matter, but things look different once you reach the ballroom. As Marianne's first partner claimed her, Poppy tried to smile and not feel bereft. The only other ladies not dancing were elderly chaperones. Lord Richard and Lady Margaret, who loved to dance, had taken to the floor once Poppy assured them that she was all right.

But she wasn't all right.

She was surrounded by women who smelled of lavender water (a scent she had always detested), and all around the room people were staring at her and whispering behind their hands. In Westfalin, ringed by her eleven sisters, she did not attract

much attention. But here in Breton, a visiting foreign princess was the subject of much gossip. A visiting foreign princess who refused to dance for unknown reasons was even more interesting.

Lady Thwaite, freed from the reception line, came over to Poppy a few moments later. "Your Highness, may I present the Duchess of Hinterdale?" Lady Thwaite indicated the woman at her side, who was shaped rather alarmingly like the prow of a ship.

Poppy shook the woman's hand. "How do you do?"

"Veddy, veddy well," the duchess replied, staring down her remarkable nose at Poppy.

Lady Thwaite went off to see to the rest of her guests, leaving Poppy and the duchess to make each other's acquaintance. The duchess spoke in a drawling fashion that forced Poppy to listen very carefully. She had studied Bretoner since she was three, but her governess had always used perfect grammar and pronunciation.

Unlike the Duchess of Hinterdale.

"You are a strenge gel, Princessss Puppy," the duchess said. "He-ere you are, with ev-er-y young man in Breton to dence with you, and you well not dence."

"Ah," Poppy said after deciphering this. "No. I don't den—dance."

"Wuh-hy not?" The duchess raised one overplucked eyebrow.

"Because my mother and sisters and I were cursed to dance for the pleasure of an evil king," Poppy thought. She reached

up and straightened her knitted silk choker. "I do not care for dancing," she said finally.

"Do not care for dencing?" The duchess's face was abruptly purple. "My godson was Prence Alllfred!" And with that the Duchess of Hinterdale stormed off, leaving Poppy with burning cheeks and a hammering heart.

"Alfred," Poppy muttered under her breath. "Duel? Or horse accident? He was the horsy one . . . yes." She put one hand over her eyes, then snatched it away, knowing that people were watching her and whispering behind their fans.

Alfred, King Rupert's late son, had gone to Westfalin to find out the secret of their ruined dancing slippers, failed, and returned to Breton to die in some sort of accident a week later. He had been foolish and vain, but no worse than a lot of spoiled princes.

And it was because of Alfred that Poppy had been sent to Breton. In the wake of his son's death, King Rupert had stirred up rumors of witchcraft and foul play at the Westfalin court, which even now continued to circulate.

But since the mystery of the slippers had been solved (even though the solution had not been widely broadcast), and three uneventful years had passed, Rupert and Gregor had reached an uneasy truce and Rupert had come up with this grand fostering program to establish stronger ties among the Ionian nations.

The first to be taken from her home and family? Poppy. In an effort to appease his royal neighbors, Gregor had volunteered all

of his unmarried daughters. Poppy and Daisy had asked to go together, but no one seemed to want two of the mysterious Westfalian princesses at once. It had been a wrench, leaving her twin behind, but she didn't envy Daisy, who had pulled Venenzia out of the hat.

Daisy hated boats, and humid air made her hair frizz, and the streets of Venenzia were paved with water. Her first letter to Poppy had been a hysterical recitation of horrors, from her wild hair to the shaky gondolas to the food, though Poppy argued that Bretoner cuisine was far worse.

"Are you all right?" A tall young man saw her shudder and strode over to her. It was Richard "but everyone calls me Dickon" Thwaite, the genial eighteen-year-old son of her host and hostess.

Poppy blurted out, "I was just thinking about kippers and blood sausage," and then bit her lip, feeling like a fool.

Dickon took a step back, startled. "I see. Well. I thought you might be bored, sitting alone here, but it seems that you are more than capable of entertaining yourself." He gave a little bow and started to move on. He had been hovering near Poppy's chair, waiting to talk to Marianne, whom he had already danced with twice.

"Wait!" Poppy stretched out a hand. She *was* bored, and more self-conscious than she'd ever imagined she could be, and she didn't want to have another encounter with another indignant matron like the Duchess of Hinterdale.

"Yes, Your Highness?"

"Er, where are you going now?"

He paused. "Well, since Marianne's dance card is full now and you are occupied with important thoughts about breakfast meats, I thought I might take myself to the card room for a hand or two." He nodded in the direction of a little door to one side of the ballroom. Through it, Poppy could see part of a table occupied by four men, deep in their game.

"I shall join you," she told him with relief. She got to her feet and took his arm before she saw the shocked expression on his face. "What is the matter?"

"Young ladies don't . . . I shouldn't really . . . ," he spluttered.

"Oh, nonsense! I love to play cards."

And Poppy steered him out of the ballroom and into the rather smoky little card room, where their appearance briefly stopped all conversation. She felt a flush of regret: apparently young ladies really *didn't* play cards.

"Ah, Poppy dear," Lord Richard said, coming to her rescue. "Care to join me?" He had been standing to one side, talking to a friend and watching a game that looked to be ending. "Poppy and young Thwaite and I will take this table next, if you don't mind, Robert. And perhaps Geoffrey will consent to make up the fourth."

The men all agreed despite their shock at seeing a young lady in their midst, and got up as soon as the hand was finished. Robert, the winner, gathered up his chips with a bemused expression.

"Didn't think you played anymore, Seadown," he said.

"Ah, well, a hand or two with my lovely houseguest hardly counts as gambling deep," Lord Richard said airily.

Poppy could tell by the look in his eyes and the surprised way that many of the men in the room were staring at Lord Richard that it was a weightier matter than he made it seem. She wondered if he had come to grief because of cards in the past. She wondered, too, if she ought to let him win.

Before marrying her two oldest sisters, Poppy's brothers-in-law had both been common soldiers. They had taught the girls a number of things: to shoot a rifle and a pistol, make a fire, knit, cook stew, sing all twenty-eight verses of "Baden-Baden Mädchen," and play a number of card games not normally enjoyed by young ladies.

It came as quite a surprise to her family when Poppy proved to be fairly adept at knitting. It did not surprise them, however, when she also turned out to be the best card player in the bunch. Although Poppy's gambling had proved far less dangerous than Petunia's fascination with bonfires, which had resulted in her chopping up one of King Gregor's prize rosebushes for kindling.

Sitting down at the table, Poppy unbuttoned her gloves and folded them back so she could handle the cards better. She shuffled and dealt while Geoffrey and Dickon Thwaite stared in amazement. Lord Richard just chuckled.

"The princess is an uncommon young lady, you will find," he told the others. "Oh, and forgive my manners! Poppy, this is the Honorable Geoffrey Wainwright. Geoffrey, this is Princess Poppy of Westfalin."

"Charmed," the Honorable Geoffrey murmured.

"Shall we set a minimum bid, gentlemen?" Poppy picked up her cards and arranged them.

"Let's keep it small, shall we?" Lord Richard also situated his hand, and the other two scrambled to pick up their cards. "Otherwise Margaret will think I'm corrupting the innocent."

Poppy glowered a bit at this, but Lord Richard just laughed. "Not you, my dear. But young Thwaite has only had a year at university."

Now it was "young Thwaite's" turn to glower.

Poppy sighed, realizing that it was up to her to break the heavy mood in the card room.

"First bid?"

Guest

And this is the portrait hall," Prince George said.

"Very nice," Christian agreed, and tried not to yawn.

He'd traveled for two days to reach the Bretoner capital of Castleraugh, and when he'd arrived George had insisted on giving Christian a guided tour of Tuckington Palace. Christian had seen more portraits of unfortunately horse-faced Bretoners than he cared to remember, and passed more inviting chairs and sofas than he could bear. At that very moment they were standing two paces away from a silk-upholstered couch littered with small round cushions, and Christian thought he could hear it whispering enticingly to him.

"This armor belonged to my great-great-great-grandfather, King Gerald," George was saying. Then he frowned at the plaque affixed to the pedestal the armor stood on. "No, wait. It was my great-great-great-great-uncle, Prince Everard's." George pulled at his lower lip. "I could have sworn it was Gerald's," he muttered. "What's become of Gerald's kit, then?"

Christian swayed on his feet and then pinched himself to stay awake. "George," he interrupted the prince's musing, trying not to stare at the couch. "Do you suppose we might take the tour in the direction of my room? I hate to admit it, but I'm exhausted. Perhaps I could see the portraits another time."

Blinking, George looked from Christian to the armor and back. "All right," he said finally, clearly flummoxed by this lack of interest in Prince Everard's breastplate and greaves. "Let me show you our guest rooms."

Apparently, when Prince George was in the mood to give a tour, nothing would deter him. On their way to Christian's room George led him through a number of other chambers, listing the famous guests who had stayed there over the years. When they at last reached the "Blue Room" assigned to Christian, which had once housed a Shijnren empress, they caught a little maid in the act of laying the fire.

"Oh, I beg your pardon, Your Highnesses!" She scrambled to her feet and curtsied. She had frizzy red hair under a white linen cap and a smudge of soot on her nose.

Christian tapped his own nose. "You have a smut," he told her kindly. She turned bright red, dropped the basket she had been carrying the kindling in, snatched it up again, and backed out of the room with more apologies.

"Of course she had a smut," George said, laughing. "She's a *maid.* The question is: why hadn't she laid the fire earlier, sparing us the sight of seeing her and her smut?" He shook his head in exasperation. "Still, we've had worse . . . that dark-haired one . . ." He shuddered.

The Dane court was a good deal more casual, Christian reflected, shedding his coat and flopping into a chair by the hearth. At home the maids came and went whether or not he was in the room, and Fru Jensen, the housekeeper, had scolded him a number of times for tracking mud on the carpet or mussing a freshly made bed. Breton was going to take a great deal of getting used to.

Not the least of which was because of George.

"Ball tonight," George said, taking the other hearthside seat. "Duke of Laurence, so we'd best make an appearance."

Glancing at the clock, Christian stifled a groan. He'd have to start dressing in an hour if they were to attend a ball, and he was so tired the room was swimming.

"Perhaps you could give my excuses to the duke," Christian said. "I really am done in by my journey—"

"Nonsense," said George. "I've already told Laurence you'd be there. I'll have some tea and scones sent up for now. Very restorative, tea and scones." And George left.

Since this was not the Danelaw and Fru Jensen was not here to scold him, Christian threw himself facedown on the bed with his boots on. He'd been looking forward to having Prince George around for the first few weeks of his visit; another young man of the same rank would be interesting to talk to. But having just spent three hours in George's company, Christian couldn't wait for him to depart. Christian buried his head in a pillow and tried to erase the portrait of George's great-grandmother, the dowager queen Louisa, and her mustache from his mind.

He managed a whole hour of sleep before Prince George's valet woke him. While Christian stumbled about in tired befuddlement, the man silently found his evening clothes and helped Christian dress, even combing his hair for him.

Before he knew it, Christian was a guest of honor at the Duke of Laurence's Harvest Ball. As soon as they had greeted their hosts, he found a chair and sank into it, waving off George, who turned away without any evidence of regret and positively threw himself at a knot of giggling young ladies.

Christian yawned and looked around. A dance was starting, and George was leading a tall blonde to the floor. Other couples followed, except for a black-haired girl across from him. Despite the lively music and the fact that there was plenty of space on the floor for another couple, the young woman did not get up to dance. Christian decided she must have too many suitors to choose from, and turned to look around the room.

The Duke of Laurence's mansion was huge, and the ballroom ran the width of the house, looking out over the gardens at the back. He could see through an open door into the supper room, where the tables had been laid for what he hoped was a splendid feast. The scones he'd gulped while dressing were nothing but a fond memory now.

"No card room, if that's what Your Highness is looking for," said the duke gruffly.

Christian looked up to see his host standing over him with a young woman on his arm.

"The wife and I disapprove of gambling," the duke explained, frowning at Christian.

"Oh, no, I was just . . . admiring your home," he said lamely.

"Forget the house, admire the ladies!" The duke gestured to the girl on his arm. "Marianne, this is His Royal Highness Prince Christian of the Danelaw. Prince Christian, this is Lady Marianne Seadown. There, you're introduced; ask Marianne to dance."

Christian felt his ears grow hot, and was mollified to see that Lady Marianne was also blushing. He hadn't planned on dancing, but he didn't want to embarrass anyone either. He stood and took her arm.

"This dance is almost finished," she said timidly, looking down at the toes of her slippers. "Shall we take a turn about the room until it is over?"

"That would be fine," he agreed.

"Here, speed things up for you," the duke said. He stalked over to the corner where the orchestra sat and shouted, "We've done with that tune, start the next!"

"The duke is very . . . ," Christian began.

"Blunt?" Marianne smiled as her blushes faded.

"I was going to say loud, but blunt would work as well."

"I swear I didn't put him up to it," she said as they took their places for the next dance, a *valse*.

"I believe you," he told her.

As they twirled around the floor, he caught a glimpse of the black-haired girl again. She was still sitting in her chair by the wall, though she had fewer suitors this time. She didn't even tap her foot to the music, but sat with a frozen look of

polite interest on her face. Christian noticed that she had no dance card dangling from her wrist, and wondered if she were crippled.

"Looking at Poppy?" Marianne raised a dark brow. "Quite a stunner, I know! I'll never compete!"

"You are quite beautiful," he said, the compliment coming easily to his lips. It helped that it was true. "I just wondered why she doesn't dance. She's the only young lady sitting out."

"Poppy doesn't dance," Marianne confided. "Ever." She studied his face, making Christian uncomfortable. "Don't you know who she is? She's from Westfalin . . . ?"

Christian stumbled and nearly tripped over Marianne's feet. When they recovered he said, "Is she one of *those* princesses?"

Marianne's face hardened. "There's no need to say it that way," she told him. "Poppy is my second cousin, you know."

"I'm terribly sorry, I meant no offense." Christian heartily wished he'd been able to get some sleep earlier. He felt incredibly slow-witted and was afraid he was going to trip again, with his tongue or his feet. "It's just that I'd heard about the . . . slippers . . . and that one of . . . the Westfalin princesses would be here too."

In fact, it had nearly kept his father from sending him. When the letter outlining the travel arrangements had arrived, King Rupert had mentioned that one of his cousin's daughters would also be present. He had probably meant to show how generous and peaceable he was, but it had alarmed King Karl to no end.

"Witches loose in Castleraugh!" Karl had ranted. "You

cannot go!" It was only when his wife and Christian had both pointed out that to back out now would insult both Westfalin and Breton, and perhaps cause the very international breach that this heir-swapping was to prevent, that he calmed down.

"Poppy says she's worn out enough dancing slippers for five lifetimes," Marianne said. "So she never dances." She gave a little laugh, which let Christian know that his unintentional insult had been forgiven. "If there's a card room, though, she usually plays."

"Really?" He wondered if it were different here in Breton—back home the card rooms at balls were only for the gentlemen.

"It's quite shocking," Marianne assured him, guessing at his expression. "But she says there's no point in being a wall-flower when she can earn some pin money off the gentlemen."

"Is she good at cards?"

"I don't think she's ever lost a hand," Marianne told him, as proud as if she were the one who'd taught her cousin to play.

"Really?" Christian decided that he wouldn't mind meeting this odd Westfalian princess. She didn't look at all like a witch, nor did she sound like the scheming heartbreaker he'd expected.

But he never got a chance to meet Poppy that night. Since George had insisted they arrive fashionably late, the *valse* with Marianne turned out to be the supper dance, so he escorted her in to the meal. It was quite sumptuous, and Marianne was good company. After supper he did his duty by dancing with the Laurence granddaughters.

After the third (rather bucktoothed) young Lady Laurence,

Christian sat down by a window to catch his breath. He dozed for a time, something that would embarrass him later when he could think more clearly. What woke him was the sound of a struggle, followed by a young woman's voice saying, "Get away from me, you fool!"

He sat up straight and looked around, finally locating the sound as coming from the garden behind him. There was no door in sight, and he was still somewhat groggy, so he simply went to the open window and half-leaped, half-fell out of it.

Christian landed on top of a burly young man who swore and punched him in the ear. He had a dim recollection of a bluish white skirt flickering away as the young lady ran off, and then a better punch from the burly young man connected with his nose and he lost consciousness.

Gossip

When the strange young man fell out of the window and started to fight Jasper Antwhistle, Poppy went to find a stick. She had no interest in getting a black eye trying to separate them, and their flailing around made it very likely. She thought that a fallen tree branch would be just the thing to jab at them until they separated.

Unfortunately, the Laurence garden was so well tended that there were no loose sticks lying around, and the fight had ended by the time she had gone into the ballroom and borrowed a walking stick from an amused older gentleman. There was quite a crowd gathered around the pair. The window-leaper was out cold, with blood streaming from his nose, and Antwhistle was claiming that he had been attacked without provocation.

Poppy did not quite know what to do. If she admitted that she had been in the garden with Antwhistle she would be branded a flirt or worse. But she didn't want whoever this poor boy on the grass was to get the blame, either.

Then it turned out that he was a prince.

"Thank heavens," she sighed to Marianne in the carriage on the way home. "One of the privileges of royalty: everyone wants to think the best of you."

"Unless they don't like you," Marianne pointed out, accidentally reminding Poppy of the accusations against her family.

"Well, in this case they liked him," she said, wincing.

Once the young man had been identified as the newly arrived Prince Christian, everyone had been more than willing to suggest that it had merely been an accident. Prince George claimed to have seen Christian dozing in a chair by the window, then suddenly wake and leap out that same window.

So the visiting prince was deemed overtired by his journey. He was given a cold compress and a cup of tea, and then sent back to Tuckington Palace to get some rest.

"All in all a most satisfactory evening," Marianne announced.

Poppy had to laugh. "It ended with us standing in the garden, looking over an unconscious prince and a red-faced Jasper Antwhistle." She paused, making sure that Lady Margaret was asleep before continuing. "Who was attacked, rather haphazardly, by Prince Christian after I slapped him for trying to kiss me and pinch my bottom at the same time."

Marianne gasped, then giggled, and Poppy joined in.

The girls laughed all the way home to Seadown House. Lord Richard was waiting for them. He had had some out-of-town business to conduct, and was only just arriving home himself.

"Did you dance with all the handsome lads, my sweeting?" He chucked Marianne under the chin.

"A few." She smiled. "Including the newly arrived Dane prince."

"Who also escorted her to supper," Poppy added.

"Is that so?" Lord Richard gave his daughter a searching look. "Don't force yourself to fall in love with him just because he's a prince," he warned Marianne.

She rolled her eyes. "Please, Papa! If I had any romantic notions about princes, Cousin George cured me of them long ago!"

"Good." Lord Richard turned to Poppy next. "And you, my fine little cardsharp? Did you fill your purse this evening?"

Poppy made a face and held a dramatic hand to her forehead. "Alas, the Laurences do not hold with gambling, so there was no card room," she said. "I was forced to make small talk all night. That is, until Prince Christian fell out a window onto one of my bravos and ended the evening."

As a result of this remark, Poppy and Marianne were up until dawn telling Marianne's parents what had happened in the garden. Lady Margaret had been busy talking with some of the other chaperones, so she had heard the commotion but hadn't known what it was about.

The girls omitted, by silent agreement, any mention of Antwhistle getting fresh with Poppy. Instead they merely said that Poppy and Antwhistle had gone for a walk in the garden, and that a bad dream the prince had had while dozing had led

him to believe that Poppy needed rescuing. The adults gave them narrow looks, as if suspicious that certain events were being glossed over, but let it go.

Poppy found herself in her bedroom at last. She was sitting in her nightgown brushing out her hair when the oil lamp at her elbow suddenly flickered green. She looked down at it, but it was yellow again. She went back to brushing her hair and then climbed into bed.

She dreamed that she was back in the Palace Under Stone, being forced to dance until her feet bled.

As she whirled around the floor in Prince Blathen's too-tight grip, she railed at him, using every swear word she could think of, but he just grinned down at her. She managed to free herself and looked for something to fight him with. She picked up a walking stick, the same one she had borrowed earlier, and whacked her erstwhile suitor with it. He crumbled to dust, but another prince took his place, and another and another.

"No," she shouted. "No, no, no! You're dead, and I will never dance again."

The King Under Stone himself rose to face her. "Poppy, my flower," he said. "You *will* dance again, and again, and again. You will never be free of us. We are your true family."

He stretched out his arms to embrace her, and suddenly there was a crowd of strange people around him all reaching for Poppy as well. Their skin was too white and their smiles were cruel; some were old and some very young, and some grew steadily less human and more monstrous. She tried to

run, but her feet were stuck to the stone floor. She raised her skirts and looked down at them. Her shoes were melting, gluing her to the floor.

"Noooo!"

Sweating, Poppy sat bolt upright in bed and looked around. The room was dark, and empty, and she didn't want to lie down again. She put on her dressing gown and slippers and went down to the kitchen to see if she could make some sweet tea.

"Oh, Your Highness!" Mrs. Hanks, the housekeeper, struggled to her feet. She was sitting at the big table in the middle of the kitchen with another plump woman in an apron, who also stood and curtsied.

"Hello," Poppy said. Seeing a strong resemblance between the two women, she asked, "Sisters?"

"Yes," they said at the same time.

Poppy felt a wash of homesickness. She had never spent so many nights away from her twin. She wondered how Daisy was faring and if sometimes they were thinking of each other at the exact same moment.

Then she realized that Mrs. Hanks and her sister were staring at her, and made an effort to drag her mind back to the here and now. They were standing on each side of the table, their hands clutching at their starched aprons.

"Anything I can get for you, Your Highness?" Mrs. Hanks said at last. She and her sister shared a look. "With the Laurence's ball going until the wee hours, we didn't think anyone would notice if Louise snuck away to have a little chat."

"Oh, of course," Poppy said. "I just came in for some tea. Please, keep visiting. I shan't tell a soul."

They smiled at her and Mrs. Hanks's sister sat back down. Mrs. Hanks, however, hurried to the stove and fixed Poppy a cup of peppermint tea, despite Poppy's assurances that she could do it herself.

"So." Feeling awkward, Poppy looked at Mrs. Hanks's sister, Mrs. Mills. "Are you also . . ." She had to think of what they called it here in Breton. "In service?"

"Yes, I'm the head housekeeper at Tuckington Palace," Mrs. Mills said with real pride.

Poppy could see why and she gave a low whistle of appreciation. "That must be . . . hectic."

"It is, that's why we have to sneak a visit whenever we can," said Mrs. Hanks. She bustled over to the table and gave Poppy her tea, a bowl of sugar, and a plate of biscuits.

Never one to turn away free food, Poppy ate three biscuits immediately. Then she stirred sugar into the fragrant peppermint tea while listening to the two older women.

"She's a real trial, Jane," Mrs. Hanks's sister was saying. "Can't do a lick of work without breaking, spilling, or burning something. That's why I couldn't keep her with me, not at the palace! And now she's about to be turned out of another place—her third!"

"Poor child," Mrs. Hanks clucked. "I know she wasn't born to it, but hasn't she had enough experience by now?"

Mrs. Mills heaved a huge sigh. "That's what makes it so hard. She can't seem to do anything right, but if you correct

her, she just cries. It's easier to clean up the mess yourself, but there's not many housekeepers as will put up with it."

Poppy couldn't stand it anymore. "Pardon me for eavesdropping, but who are you talking about?"

Mrs. Hanks and Mrs. Mills exchanged looks.

"Please? I won't tell another soul," Poppy wheedled. "Except Daisy and maybe Rose and Galen and Lily and Orchid," she added to herself, but they weren't in Breton so it hardly mattered.

Mrs. Mills leaned closer over the table. "Well, Your Highness, before I was at the palace I was the housekeeper for an earl's family. They had a daughter named Eleanora, just a darling little thing with dark hair like yours, but blue eyes." She smiled in reminiscence, and then her face clouded. "But the earl's luck turned sour overnight. First they had to sell their beautiful country estate, then they sold most of the furniture in the town house. They let the staff go one by one, including me." Her eyes were shiny with tears.

"Still," she went on in a choked voice. "My lady was so good to me. She helped me get on at the palace. I was an underhousekeeper at first, but I've moved up smart enough." She took a sip of her own tea. "Two years later, they lost everything. The earl died of apoplexy, and my lady of heartbreak." A tear rolled down her plump cheek, and Mrs. Hanks put a hand on her sister's arm. "Oh, silly me!" She wiped her face with the corner of her apron. "A month later, who should knock on the kitchen door but my own little Eleanora, without a friend

in the world but me. I got her a job as an upstairs maid where I could keep an eye on her . . . ," she trailed off.

"But that girl," Mrs. Hanks finished for her sister, her voice hard. "That girl, who now insists on being called Ellen because it's more 'common sounding,' has caused nothing but trouble. Sulking, ruining things, shirking her duties, and quitting jobs or being fired!" She gave her sister's arm a squeeze. "You always were more patient than I, Louise. I'd have boxed the girl's ears and set her to peeling potatoes in the scullery if she'd given me a tenth of that trouble."

Poppy rather agreed with Mrs. Hanks. She'd often wondered what would happen to her if she was disowned (something her father frequently threatened). She had watched the maids, and decided that she could probably make a go of it. She certainly wouldn't beg help from someone and then treat her the way this Eleanora/Ellen was treating Mrs. Hanks's poor sister.

"Mrs. Shields, the Laurences' housekeeper," the sister said, having composed herself, "says that if she makes one more mistake, she's out on the street for sure. They made her hide in the scullery during the ball, so she wouldn't accidentally injure a guest or set the house on fire!"

"If she's sacked just send her here," Mrs. Hanks said. "I'll give her a job."

Poppy finished her tea in silence, wondering how soon Ellen would be working for the Seadowns, and if she was really as horrible as Mrs. Hanks made her out to be.

Odd

Ahem, ahem, Your Highness?"

By now Christian was so used to the red-haired maid's skittishness that he didn't look up from the letter he was writing. Despite her years serving the Bretoner royal family, she seemed to find Christian highly intimidating.

"Put it on the table, please," he said, and went on describing the opera he had seen the night before. He was writing to the oldest of his sisters, ten-year-old Margrete, and he knew that she would want each act described in detail.

The sound of an entire tea tray falling to the hearth was too much to ignore, however.

"What in the world?" He dropped his quill and turned to see the girl standing in the middle of a pile of broken china, tears welling from her eyes.

"Oh, Your Highness! I'm so sorry!" She pointed to the puddle of tea. "It looked green!"

"Green?" He frowned at the brown liquid.

"I thought . . . it glowed . . . just for a moment. I was so startled!"

"Glowed green? That is odd." He shrugged. "It looks fine now, though. Here, I'll help you gather it up."

She turned bright red and gave a little laugh, wiping her eyes with her apron. "No, no, Your Highness! I'm not half so bad as Ellen; Mrs. Mills won't sack me over this."

"Ellen?"

"Oh, a maid from a few years back," the girl chattered, now suddenly at ease with him as they squatted by the hearth and gathered up the shards of china. She mopped up the tea with a napkin and wrung it out in the remains of the pot. "She broke everything she touched; it was awful. Mrs. Mills gave her second and third chances, but Their Majesties found out and she was fired."

"I see," Christian said. He handed her the tray, and she bobbed a curtsy and went out.

"I'll be right back," she promised.

When he turned around he saw a green gleam, just like the maid had said. This one came from the oil lamp on his writing desk. He went over to tweak the wick, and the flame was yellow and orange as it always was. As he fiddled with it, it guttered and smoked and went out. He needed to finish his letter, but the lamp wouldn't relight. The wick felt slick and cold, and the oil in the cut glass bowl was oddly discolored.

Christian rang for a footman, who brought him a new

lamp and reminded him that it was almost time for his ride with the princesses. Putting aside the letter to his sister with a sigh, he changed into riding clothes.

~

An hour later he heard the name Ellen again, brought up this time by one of the princesses. George was busy packing for his trip to Spania, so it fell to Christian to supervise the princesses' daily riding expedition, along with the help of two grooms. He was thinking that his own sisters were not this much trouble as Princess Hermione, age eight, tumbled off her pony into a hedge for the third time.

"Don't be such an Ellen," Emmeline said to her little sister with great superiority. She was eleven, but had the mannerisms of a young lady twice her age.

"An Ellen?" Christian raised his eyebrows, puzzled.

Both princesses erupted in laughter.

"She was our maid," Emmeline explained through her giggles. "And she was so clumsy! Quite, quite ridiculous!"

Christian frowned at them. "You shouldn't laugh at someone just because she's clumsy," he told them. He was supposed to be making friends with the Bretoner royal family, but since Emmeline had announced that she would marry him when she turned twelve, he had done his best to seem old and boring and stern.

"But she really was awful," Hermione said. "She broke the pillows."

"How do you break a pillow?"

Emmeline rolled her eyes. "She didn't really *break* the pillows, she ripped the cases; there were feathers everywhere. She burned everything she ironed, and she tripped while bringing me hot chocolate and it spilled all over my nightgown *four* times."

"She combed my hair once," Hermione added, "and when she was done there were *more* tangles in it. I don't know how she did it, but she did."

"It was clearly on purpose," Emmeline said with authority. "Then she cried so that people would feel sorry for her. Fat old Millsy said to give her more time, but Mother said no."

Christian wondered how the girl had gotten a place at the palace to begin with. "Don't call Mrs. Mills fat, it's rude," he said finally, and led them across the grounds.

His eyes were bothering him. The palace grounds, both lawns and shrubbery, seemed dull and dry even though the Tuckington Palace gardens were renowned throughout Ionia. Yet at the same time he saw green sparkles in the corners of his vision. He rubbed at his eyes, and heard someone laughing.

"What is so amusing?" He turned to frown at Emmeline. She gave him a quizzical look. "Odd," he muttered under his breath.

"What did you say?" Emmeline had her eyebrows raised, and her expression gave Christian hope that her infatuation with him was cooling.

"Nothing," he said, and swiped at his eyes again. "Nothing."

Maid

Ellen Parker sat on the narrow cot in her new room at Seadown House and closed her eyes for just a moment. Soon the Seadowns's housekeeper, Mrs. Hanks, would come in to tell her the house rules, to tell her that she should be grateful, to tell her that she was just a maid.

Ellen's proud heart shrank a little more, and she wished that she had a few tears left to cry. She had sobbed all the way from the Laurences's manor and didn't think that there was a single drop of moisture left in her. She took out a thin handkerchief and rubbed at the salt stains on her cheeks.

"Hacks are so filthy, aren't they?" Mrs. Hanks said as she came in. "The pitcher's full, if you need to freshen up."

"Thank you, ma'am," Ellen said woodenly. Mrs. Hanks looked very much like her sister, and despite Ellen's fond feelings for Mrs. Mills, she had found little comfort with her.

"Now, Ellen," Mrs. Hanks began, her voice firm.

"Here comes the lecture," thought Ellen. "At least she

remembered to use my new name." The former Eleanora Parke-Whittington found it painful to be reminded of her past by being called Eleanora, and so she had altered her name to something more in keeping with her altered status. She had been named after her grandmother, and that leader of fashion had never had to empty her own chamber pot, let alone anyone else's.

"I know that you were not born to this work, my dear, but then I don't know of anyone who would have chosen it. I would rather be served than a servant myself!" Mrs. Hanks smiled but Ellen just looked away. The smile would fade soon enough, when it became apparent that Ellen was useless. "We'll do the best that we can to help you, but you have been in service now for some years, and I expect you to be able to do some things without supervision."

Ellen just nodded, and out of the corner of her eye she saw Mrs. Hanks's smile thin out. "Yes, ma'am," she said hastily.

"I will introduce you to His Lordship in an hour, though most of your duties will be with the young ladies of the household, Lady Marianne and Her Highness Princess Poppy of Westfalin." Mrs. Hanks swelled a bit with importance when she said the princess's name.

"Yes, ma'am," Ellen said, her voice barely audible. She hadn't realized that she would be waiting on girls her own age, girls who would have been her friends if things had gone differently.

It seemed that she did have tears left to cry after all.

"Here is a dress that should fit," Mrs. Hanks laid a bundle

on the bed. "Apron and cap as well. We can alter them later if there is any need. The black stockings and shoes you have on will be just fine. I'll let you get freshened up," Mrs. Hanks said, not noticing Ellen's distress—and who cared if a maid was upset? The plump housekeeper went out, closing the door behind her.

Steeling herself, Ellen went to the washstand, trying to avoid her reflection in the dim little looking glass that hung above it. There was a bouquet of dried flowers hanging next to the mirror, belonging to the maid that Ellen would share the narrow room with. At least they would not have to share a bed: there were two cots, thank heavens. And the basin and pitcher, though plain, were not cracked or chipped. The servants quarters at the Laurences' were furnished with things too damaged to be used in the more visible parts of the house.

She lifted the pitcher and poured water into the basin. As it ran into the white porcelain, the water turned green. Ellen nearly dropped the heavy pitcher, only just managing to put it back on the table in time. From the glowing green water, she heard a kindly voice speaking.

"Poor dear! All alone in the world, aren't you?"

Ellen whirled around, but the door was still closed and there wasn't another soul in the room. "Who said that?" Her voice came out thin and shaky.

"They call me the Corley," the voice said. "But I am also your godmother, my dear. Pour more water into the pitcher, that I may see you."

"What?"

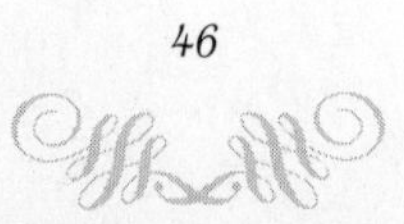

"When you pour water, I can see you," the voice said, still patient and soft. It was a plump voice, a gentle voice, the voice of a grandmother in a lace cap and woolen shawl. "Pour the water, dear Eleanora, and let us talk."

Still shaking, Ellen picked up the pitcher again.

Dancer

Purl two, knit four, purl two, knit four," Poppy muttered under her breath. She gave her yarn a tug to unspool more.

"Step two, three, now entrechat," said the dancing master, and brought his long cane down with a *crack* on the wooden floor.

At the cue, Marianne leaped into the air, clicked her heels together, and then landed with a thump. She wavered for a moment, nearly fell, and regained her balance with an embarrassed burst of laughter.

"Stand straight," the dancing master barked. Mirth fled from Marianne's face and she threw her shoulders back. "Again," the man said. "Step two, three, and entrechat!"

Marianne leaped and flapped her feet and did her best to land with grace and dignity. As Poppy sat in the corner, dividing her attention between her knitting and Marianne's lesson, she reflected that she had gotten off easy. Since Poppy did not dance, there was no need to disgrace herself trying to learn the strange new Analousian steps that were all the rage. They were part ballet, part acrobatics, and even the normally graceful Marianne was having trouble. Poppy thought that she could master the entrechat and a few of the other steps with a minimum of effort—after a decade of experience, she could dance on the steeple of a church if she wanted to—but she was thrilled to not have to.

"Oof!" Marianne, temporarily released from her lesson, flounced into the chair beside Poppy. "I don't think it's going to look very attractive at the next ball, if the new dances make me all red and sweaty."

"I'm sure that Dickon Thwaite will find you all the more lovely with a red face," said Poppy mischievously.

"What was that?" Marianne looked at her, face even redder.

"Nothing." Poppy turned back to her knitting.

"What *is* that?" Marianne leaned in closer.

"I was just joking," Poppy began, then saw that Marianne was looking at the tube of blue wool dangling from her hands. "Oh, it's a bed sock."

"For whom? It's enormous!"

Poppy held up the sock, which was almost as large and as long as a sweater sleeve. "It will shrink in the wash, and be just the right size for you," she told Marianne. "Truly."

"You'd best let Ellen wash it then, if you *want* it to shrink." She rolled her eyes.

"She's trying," Poppy said.

"I don't think she is," Marianne argued. "She looked almost happy when she told me yesterday that my new shawl was ruined."

Poppy sighed. "It's true," she said, rueful. She wanted to give the new maid the benefit of the doubt, but Mrs. Hanks had been correct: the girl seemed to be purposefully inept, and showed no interest whatsoever in learning how to perform her tasks correctly.

Clothing she took to mend or iron came back with larger tears and more creases. Every fire she laid smoked and sputtered, every tray she carried rattled until tea spilled or buns rolled off onto the floor. You could hear her coming by the clatter of dishes, and see where she was going by following the trail of broken china or crumpled stockings.

"I certainly hope she doesn't lose her position here," Poppy said, absently counting stitches. "I don't know of anyone else who would hire her, and what other work could she find? If she tried the theater, she'd probably bring the whole set crashing down."

Marianne snickered, which made Poppy feel a bit guilty. She hadn't been joking, not really. Ellen was so hopeless at being a maid that Poppy had indeed turned her mind to other careers for the girl, and couldn't think of a thing she was suited for.

Still snickering, Marianne got back up to practice her dancing again. She stood in the middle of the ballroom, looking stiff and awkward, and then leaped straight up. When she came down hard, she gave a little shriek. "My feet!"

Without thinking about it, Poppy tossed aside her knitting and went over to her. "You landed flat-footed," she scolded. "And the way you're standing is giving me a crick in the spine. Do it like this."

Throwing back her head and shoulders, Poppy bent her knees just slightly, jumped up and clicked her heels, then landed lightly on the balls of her feet. She didn't stagger, didn't bruise anything, and her gown wafted around her in the exact way that it was supposed to.

"*Très magnifique!*" The Analousian dancing master had come back into the room with Lady Margaret. Both adults applauded Poppy roundly. "*Très, très magnifique, mademoiselle!*"

"Oh!" Poppy fiddled with her necklace. "I didn't really think . . . I don't really care for dancing."

"But mademoiselle *should* care for dancing," the man insisted. "Mademoiselle is very, very graceful. Put aside the knitted thing, mademoiselle, and dance!" He began to pound on the floor in time. "Dance, dance!"

"Here, I'll be the gentleman," Marianne said eagerly.

Before she could protest, Poppy found her hands seized and she blindly followed her friend through the intricate steps of a pavane. She did another entrechat, and nearly fell this time.

The pounding of the dancing master's cane and Marianne's hands grabbing at hers the moment she came down from the entrechat were making her think of the Midnight Balls of her childhood. She was wearing a blue dress, and when she caught glimpses of herself in the long mirrors on the wall of the

ballroom, it reminded her of the midnight blue gown she had worn to the last Midnight Ball. She was half-expecting her brother-in-law Galen to burst into the room, so when the door opened and a tall young man came in, she stopped so abruptly that Marianne trod on her toes.

"I hope I'm not interrupting," said the Dane prince. "I understood we were to go riding this afternoon. But if the ladies would rather dance . . ." He offered his hand to Poppy, who was too flustered to take it.

"Oh, girls, I forgot completely!" Lady Margaret clapped her hands. "His Highness asked to take you both riding, since he so enjoyed meeting Marianne and has not had time to make Poppy's acquaintance." And Lady Margaret proudly introduced Poppy to Prince Christian.

Poppy smiled politely and gathered up her knitting. "Let's go change into our riding clothes, Marianne. We won't keep you waiting long, Prince Christian."

She took Marianne's arm and hurried upstairs. Once back in her own room, she used all the best soldiers' curses she knew.

Now that they had seen her dancing and knew that she was not a hopeless stumblefoot, as so many had assumed, people would be after her to dance all the time! The Seadowns were kind, and she knew that they suspected it was some emotional pain that kept her from dancing, but Marianne was too sunny in nature to ever truly understand. And the prince? He would naturally assume that she was snubbing him if she did not dance with him at the next ball.

Her riding habit fastened in the front, which was a blessing

since her language would have scorched the ears of any maid who came to help. She got herself into it and pulled on her boots in record time. Checking in the mirror she saw that her hair looked tidy enough. She didn't have a lady's maid, and so when she needed help dressing she would have to ring the bell and take the assistance of whichever upstairs maid answered the call. It was just as likely to be the hapless Ellen as Gabrielle, Lady Seadown's formidable Analousian lady's maid, and so Poppy had been dressing herself a lot lately.

As she walked down the stairs to meet Marianne and Prince Christian, Poppy searched her feelings to decide why it was that Ellen so fascinated her. She thought it was perhaps because she wanted to pity Ellen—it would be horrible to go from a life of privilege to being a servant—but the girl's attitude made it impossible. And there was guilt, too. Guilt that she had wealth (though not as much as most princesses), guilt that her father and her sisters were still living. Yet she still could not feel completely charitable toward Ellen.

"You look a bit . . . what's the word? Oh, 'pensive,' Princess Poppy," said Prince Christian when she joined him. Marianne was still changing. "I hope that I did not offend you when I burst into the ballroom. The butler seemed to think that it would be all right."

He spoke Bretoner with a light accent not unlike Poppy's own, and had bright blue eyes and an engaging smile. Poppy found herself smiling back, her mood lifting.

"Oh no," she said, waving a hand airily. "I was thinking of something else entirely."

She studied him frankly, having no doubt that he was used to it. After all, she was. He really was handsome, she decided. Perhaps two years older than she, and his family had neither lost a son to her family's curse nor threatened violence against them during that bad time. A knot of tension in her stomach that she hadn't even known was there loosened.

"We are equals," she said, "though I am not my father's heir. Why don't you just call me Poppy." She had always thought that "Princess Poppy" sounded too much like a name for a small dog.

"And you must call me Christian," he said, giving her an even warmer smile. Yes, he was terribly handsome.

"Oh, pooh!" Marianne said as she came down the stairs. "I've taken too long and now you're dear friends and I shall be left out."

"That will teach you to spend all day primping," Poppy said, winking at Christian and taking his arm. "Five more minutes, and we would have eloped."

"I wouldn't put it past you," Marianne said, with a pretend pout. "Shall we?" And she led the way out to the drive, where Christian took in Poppy's mare with great amusement.

"Yes?" Poppy raised one eyebrow. She was not a good rider, but the Bretoners seemed to live on horseback when they were not dancing, so she was trying her best to keep up.

"Is that a horse or a large ottoman?"

"Oh hush, we can't all ride creatures like that," she retorted. He had just mounted a bay stallion with wild eyes and flared nostrils. "He looks like he might eat me."

"Best not get too close then," Christian said.

Poppy made a face at him.

The three of them rode down the street to Rother-Hythe Park, where all the fashionable folk rode. Poppy was pleased to see that she wasn't the only young lady riding a horse suitable for children and old people. Although she did notice that most of the young ladies riding such horses looked singularly brainless, and made a resolution to become a better rider.

Sensing her distraction, Christian gave her a quizzical look. "Is something wrong with your fat, elderly steed?"

"Oh," Poppy laughed. "I was thinking that it really is a shame I'm only riding this poor thing. If my brothers-in-law had been cavalry men, I'm sure I'd be jumping hedges by now."

"Your brothers-in-law?"

"I'm dying to meet them myself," Marianne said. "Galen and Heinrich sound like fun. Poppy can spit and swear and gamble like a soldier." Then a blush stained her cheeks. "And you know that I mean that in a good way, Poppy," she hastened to add.

"I know," Poppy said, blushing herself.

"Really?" A grin tugged at Christian's mouth. "So it's true that you really do play cards during balls?"

"It can get very boring, watching other people dancing," Poppy told him. She wished her fair skin didn't show her blushes so easily.

"You're a very fine dancer," Christian said in puzzlement. "I don't see why you have to watch."

Poppy winced. She knew she shouldn't have brought up

dancing again. "I don't see dancing as entertainment," she said in a low voice. "I see it as something I used to *have* to do, whether I liked it or not." She stared past Christian to the trees, briefly imagining a forest of silver, stirred by a wind that no other creature felt. At least her blush had been chased away.

"Oh," Christian said, still puzzled. "I see."

Marianne defused the tension by chiming in with the story of Poppy's first ball in Breton. "She walked right into the card room on the arm of Dickon Thwaite! Have you met Dickon, Your Highness? I mean, Christian? He's very amusing, you are sure to like him," she burbled.

"He's also very handsome, and sweet on Marianne," Poppy said out of the corner of her mouth.

"Everyone was staring," Marianne went on, ignoring Poppy. "So Papa came to her rescue and actually played some hands with them. And he hasn't touched a card in years!"

Poppy still found that puzzling. "But he's very good, and he was sitting in the card room when we went in. Are you sure he doesn't play anymore?"

"Oh, he used to play all the time," Marianne said. "And he never lost. But it bothered Mama a great deal, so he stopped." She shrugged. "Most of Papa's friends play, so he sits in the card rooms at balls to speak with them."

Christian appeared to accept this explanation readily, but Poppy still wondered about it. Lord Richard had been expert in his handling of the cards on the few occasions she had played with him. She had beaten him every time, but narrowly, and at least once she suspected that he had let her win.

This had infuriated her at the time, but now it made her curious. What had happened to Lord Richard to cause him to give up something he loved? Lady Margaret was wonderful, but her disapproval must have been harsh indeed to have had this effect. For now Poppy saw that Lord Richard didn't lose to be polite: he had lost because he truly did not want to win.

Or perhaps he was afraid to win.

Gleaming

Come in, Prince Christian, come in." King Rupert of Breton beckoned his young guest into his study.

Christian entered, bowed, and waited for the king to give him permission to sit. King Rupert was fond of ceremony and refused to drop Christian's title. In fact, his own children called him "Sire" and once Christian had heard Hermione greet her father as "Your Eminence." It made meals very stilted.

"You wished to see me, Your Majesty?" Waved to a chair, Christian sat up straight and laid his hands on the arms of the chair. His fingers wanted to trace the intricate scrollwork, but he knew that the king also hated fidgeting.

"Indeed I did, Prince Christian. Indeed I did."

The king sat behind a large desk, both hands flat on the blotter, and studied Christian. Christian smiled politely, and did not twitch or look away. He hadn't committed any crimes that he was aware of, yet a feeling of guilt took root in him all the same.

"I'm sure your royal father, King Karl, told you of the ulterior motive behind these little state visits," King Rupert said.

"Er, yes?" Christian wasn't sure what he was asking. King Rupert couldn't possibly be crass enough to talk about marriage in this way.

"So, what is your intention toward my daughters?"

Christian choked. Apparently King Rupert really *could* be that crass.

"Are you planning on marrying Hermione or Emmeline?"

"Um, I'm afraid that I haven't really . . . The girls are very young . . ." Christian felt hot and cold at the same time. If Breton was looking for an alliance through marriage, he didn't want to cause a war by refusing them outright. Why didn't Rupert take this up with Christian's father instead of ambushing him this way?

"After the New Year I believe you're to go to Analousia?"

"I think so." Christian fought to regain his composure.

"I don't want to lose you to Analousia, or Spania," Rupert said bluntly. "If they turn against us, the way Analousia went after Westfalin a few years back, you'd be forced to side with them. Hmmm." He stroked his impressive mustache. "Perhaps someone else might do." He stared into space, apparently forgetting that Christian was still in the room.

Looking at the clock, Christian realized that it was almost time to meet Marianne and Poppy at the Royal Gallery. He took a deep breath and stood, bowing. "If Your Majesty will excuse me? A certain royal duty calls."

"Yes, yes, go on, Prince Christian." King Rupert was busily jotting down notes on a piece of paper.

At the gallery, Poppy and Marianne both laughed at his panicked recital of this interview.

"Someone else?" Marianne shook her head. "I am a cousin of the royal family, but I have my cap set for my own someone else, you know." She blushed, and Christian knew she was thinking of Dickon Thwaite.

"And I'm out of the question," Poppy joked, taking his arm so that she and Marianne flanked him. "Mother was Rupert's cousin, but imagine if Father were to turn on Breton! Oh, the scandal!"

"Would your father turn on them?" Christian was only idly curious. With a girl on each arm he was getting a number of envious looks and rather enjoying them.

"Oh, heavens no!" Poppy lowered her voice. "Let's face it, King Rupert can be horrible, but Father still likes to keep on good terms with him." She sighed. "Which is why I'm here."

"Your father sent you, especially?" Christian couldn't help but think that bold Poppy was an odd choice for ambassador.

"Oh no. I drew Breton out of a hat. Hyacinth, who's very religious, is the only one who didn't draw: Father sent her to Analousia to impress them with our piety."

Christian was fascinated. "You drew lots to see who would go where?"

"No one cared which one they got," she said with a shrug. "And Lilac and Orchid both wanted to go to Spania. Some

famous actor is doing a play there this season. So Father used the hat to make things equal."

"So the twelve of you—"

"Nine," she corrected him. "Hyacinth was sent to Analousia, and Lily and Rose are married. Nobody wants a married princess," she laughed wryly.

"True." He paused. "Doesn't it bother you?"

Poppy shook her head.

"It shouldn't," Marianne put in. "Any girl with a dowry is told from the day she's born that she has to marry just the right person for just the right reasons at just the right time." She grimaced. "All you can hope for is that he's got teeth. And hair."

"Oh, don't be so put upon," Poppy said. "Your parents would never force you to marry anyone you didn't like."

They left the gallery and went out onto the grounds. The Royal Gallery was housed in a grand mansion with extensive gardens behind, which were a work of art in and of themselves. The trees had been sculpted into perfectly smooth cones, and the hedges were shaped like sea serpents and other fantastical creatures.

"Not bad," Poppy said with a critical eye. "But that yew is on its last legs."

"A gardening expert, are we?" Christian liked Poppy, but he thought she was a rather strange girl. She hated dancing but was very good at it, and meekly went riding every day despite being a terrible rider. She gambled, and could swear

quite colorfully (as he had discovered one day when the more spirited horse she was trying threw her in the park). And while she claimed to be fond of the ladylike art of knitting, the "socks" he had seen her working on were bizarrely large.

And now it seemed that she was a trained gardener.

"I don't actually care about growing anything myself," she explained. "But Father's gardens are considered the finest in Ionia. He had them created for my mother, who was terribly homesick, and at first it was only to remind her of this." She made a wide gesture with one hand to indicate the sweeping green lawns before them. "But in the end he became so involved that he's even developed a number of new roses."

"How do you develop a new rose?" Christian could barely tell the difference between a rose and a daisy.

"I really don't know." She shrugged. "But they're all named after my mother: Queen Maude, Maude's Beauty, Beloved Maude. One of my sisters asked once why Father didn't name a rose after any of us, and he pointed out what the rest of us were thinking: who names a flower 'Poppy's Rose'?"

"Daisy's Rose," Marianne put in.

Christian started to laugh, but a strange feeling came over him. It was happening with greater frequency now: the glimpses of green in the corners of his eyes, the faint sparkle in the air. It mostly happened when he was near large windows, but walking through the Mirror Gallery at the palace also made him uneasy.

He looked around and saw a small greenhouse half-hidden

behind a hedge. The glass did have a faint greenish tint, but nothing like what he thought he'd seen.

"What is it? Do they have exotic flowers?" Marianne peered toward the little house. "It looked green for a moment, but now it looks bare."

"Green? You saw it too?" Christian tried not to sound too eager. He'd thought his eyes were playing tricks again.

"I didn't see anything," Poppy said. "Except the fish in that pond there." She looked as though she were going to spear one of them with the tip of her furled parasol. Really, she was an odd girl.

"No matter," Christian said uneasily, steering them away from the greenhouse and the fish. With a note of forced casualness he asked if they cared to join him at a nearby tea shop for some refreshments.

"Of course we do," Poppy said, turning her back on the pond readily. "Young ladies are always hungry, you know, because we're not allowed to eat properly in front of potential suitors."

"What about me?" He wasn't sure if he was offended or not.

"You? But you're our friend," Poppy told him, linking her arm through his again. "Like an older brother."

"Ooh, I love strawberry icing," said Marianne. The green glass house seemed to be completely forgotten.

But Christian couldn't forget. What did it mean?

And what did Poppy mean by an "older" brother?

Invited

A week after Poppy visited the Royal Gallery with Christian and Marianne, the Seadown household received a royal invitation. They were in the breakfast room and Poppy was pretending to like kippers when it came.

The butler presented his silver tray with the thick invitation on it with great reverence, and Lady Margaret looked a bit wary as she took it. Though Her Ladyship was a cousin of the king's, royal invitations had been rather thin since Poppy arrived. The princess had been presented to King Rupert and Queen Edith, but other than that had not set foot inside the palace. Poppy hoped that her sisters were receiving warmer welcomes; from their letters that appeared to be the case.

Marianne was practically bouncing in her seat with excitement. "Will there be a gala? With fireworks?" She turned to Poppy. "It's almost the queen's birthday. Last year they had a gala, with food and music and fireworks!" Her eyes took on a dreamy look. "And Dickon Thwaite kissed me in a rose bower . . ."

Lord Richard put down his newspaper. "Young Thwaite did what?"

Marianne blushed bright pink and applied herself to her kippers. Poppy caught her host's gaze, and they both grinned.

"Whatever it is," Lord Richard said mildly as he went back to his paper, "I hope that it is properly chaperoned this time. And that there is a card room for Poppy."

Lady Margaret read the invitation twice. "This is most exciting," she said finally. "And also a bit . . . unusual."

"Tell us!" Marianne tried to snatch the invitation from her mother, who calmly held it out of her reach.

"Well, it appears that there will not just be a gala for the queen's birthday, but a masked ball two weeks later as well." Lady Margaret shook her head. "Rupert has never done something like this before."

"Rupert has never wanted a houseguest to get married so badly," Lord Richard remarked from behind the paper. "Having ties to the Danelaw's navy is nothing to sneeze at, and the princesses are too young for Christian."

"I'd best not go," Poppy said. "Seeing me will only remind everyone of Alfred, and Queen Edith detests gambling besides."

Her hosts protested, but Poppy was adamant. Upstairs, Marianne continued to pester Poppy. Poppy lay across the other girl's bed, knitting something pale blue and fuzzy.

"Don't be a goose, Poppy, you must come." Marianne was

posing in front of the mirror, sucking in her cheeks and batting her eyelashes. "What is that you're making now? Giant garters to go with the giant socks?"

"Those socks turned out beautifully, thank you very much," Poppy retorted. "Since you kept mocking them, I intend to give them to your mother at the holidays. This is a scarf."

"Ooh, for Christian?"

"For you, actually, since you mocked the bed socks," Poppy said dryly. She sat up and held the coiled blue thing against Marianne's neck. "Not with that gown, of course," she said. "It will hang down in a long curl. You'll love it, especially with your dark blue gown."

A heavy sigh preceded the maid, Ellen, as she came in. "I wish I had more than one gown," she muttered.

"You do," Poppy said shortly. "I've seen them."

Ellen gave her a baleful look. "Not nice ones."

Poppy gave up and turned her attention to her knitting. Ellen seemed to know that Mrs. Hanks would never fire her, and she used it as an excuse to address Poppy and Marianne like she was a rather depressing social acquaintance. She wasn't stupid, though, and was respectful enough whenever an adult was nearby.

"Her Ladyship says that the dressmaker will be here soon to discuss your new gowns, Lady Marianne," Ellen said. "The princess, too, if she likes." Her sour tone made it clear that she thought Poppy was a fool for not wanting a new ball gown.

Ellen stomped about the room, loudly tidying up and rearranging chairs. "Eavesdropping," Poppy thought, as Marianne

pored over her collection of magazines, looking for just the right gown.

"I want something spectacular for the masked ball," she said to Poppy. "That's going to be the really grand affair. But you'll need at least one new gown: my birthday ball will be right between the two royal parties!" She paused. "I hope everyone won't be too busy to come to my birthday."

"Of course I'll come to that," Poppy reassured Marianne. "Everyone will! I just don't know about the masquerade at the palace."

"You really should attend," Lady Margaret said, coming into the room.

"I'm not even sure that I was invited," Poppy said, looking for an excuse to get out of the royal celebrations once and for all. "If it was for the Seadown family . . . Invitations have come specifically for me in the past." She smiled inwardly, thinking that she had hit on the perfect answer.

"Actually, what it said was that 'every eligible young lady was invited along with her guardians,' " Lady Margaret gave Poppy a triumphant smile. "You happen to be an eligible young lady."

"And so am I," Ellen said.

They turned to look at her.

"I'm an eligible young lady," she said louder. She thrust her chin out. "And you know that I wasn't born a maid."

Poppy gave a low whistle. She had to admire Ellen's bravery. Sullenness was one thing, but coming right out with her grievance in front of her employer was quite another.

Lady Margaret, however, was not in the least bit nonplussed. She smiled at Ellen and gave a little nod.

"That is true, my dear," she said. "And there is no reason why you should not attend the balls. We will have some gowns—"

"I don't need your charity, thank you," Ellen interrupted, her face turning red. "I'll get my own gowns."

Dropping her knitting, Poppy leveled her gaze at Ellen. "You could be a bit more gracious!"

"It's all right, Poppy," Lady Margaret said gently, handing Poppy her needles and snarl of yarn. "If you do change your mind, Ellen, please tell me. I would be happy to help you find some suitable gowns." She smiled at the young woman.

"I don't need charity," Ellen repeated, her face cloudy.

Ellen stumped out and they could breathe again.

"You'd think she would be a little more grateful," Poppy said. That was as gracious as she could manage.

Lady Margaret shook her head. "Poor child. Life has been hard for her."

"It would be awful to go from *having* maids to *being* a maid," Marianne agreed. Then she wrinkled her nose. "But I wish she wouldn't snap at us. We're not responsible for her father's downfall!"

Poppy pursed her lips. "What if you had a ball gown made—supposedly for me—and we gave it to Ellen so it wouldn't go to waste? Since I'm not going to the gala."

"Yes, you are!" Marianne poked Poppy in the ribs.

"An interesting idea, though, Poppy," said Lady Margaret.

"I don't know where she'll get a gown otherwise. Perhaps I'll have one of Marianne's made over for her, so it doesn't seem too overbearing."

"Just don't let Ellen help," Poppy said. "It won't do her any good if she sets it on fire trying to iron out a wrinkle."

They heard a scratching sound at the door. "The dress-maker, ma'am," said the butler, and they followed him to the sitting room where the fussy little man was waiting with his pattern books and measuring tapes.

"All three of us need gowns for the upcoming royal gala and the masquerade," Lady Margaret told him. "Even Her Highness. That's in addition to the gowns we ordered for Marianne's birthday ball, of course."

"Ah, a charming pair of young ladies," the man said. "With such dark hair and fine figures, they could be sisters. And you, Lady Margaret—a third, only slightly older sister." He bowed and kissed her hand.

Poppy snorted, but she did consent to look through the book of patterns. "Who knows? I might decide to attend," she thought. "If only to keep Marianne and Dickon Thwaite out of the rose bowers."

Goddaughter

Hardly able to believe her luck, Ellen slipped back up to the narrow bedroom she shared with one of the other maids. Lady Margaret had said that she could go to the royal gala! Her Ladyship had even offered to have gowns made for her, but Ellen had another plan.

This was her chance. The foreign prince would be there; she'd seen Prince Christian when he came to call on Marianne and Poppy, and he was very handsome, and kind. Moreover, he wouldn't know about her family, about her past, and he could take her away from those who did know. Mrs. Hanks never let her wait on him, in case she spilled something on His Highness, and that was all for the good now. She wouldn't want him to recognize her at the gala.

But Ellen would need to be dazzling to draw his eye away from all the other ladies. And that meant not just a gown that had been given to her out of charity, but jewels, fans, dancing slippers, and a costume for the masked ball that would stun all who saw her. The Seadowns, despite their kindness, were unlikely to do that much. They certainly wouldn't set her up to outshine their own daughter and their beloved Poppy.

Going to the washstand, Ellen reflected that it was odd how much alike the three of them looked: Poppy, Marianne, and herself, and yet how different their circumstances were. Poppy was a princess with some sort of mysterious scandal attached to her name, Marianne was a wealthy heiress who thought of nothing but gowns and beaux, and Ellen was the daughter of an earl who found herself ironing the other girls' underclothes.

But that was all going to change. Soon.

She lifted the full pitcher and slowly began to pour water into the basin. She stared intently into the sheet of liquid as she poured.

"Madame Corley," she called. "Godmother? It's Ellen—Eleanora!"

Instantly the water turned green and the plump-cheeked face of her godmother appeared. "Hello, my darling! What is it you wanted?"

"I'm going to a ball, to *two* balls," Ellen blurted out in excitement. "And I need gowns! And slippers! And fans and jewels! Oh please, Godmother, say you can help!"

Her godmother's smile broadened. "Of course, of course, my darling girl! How happy I am for you! You shall have the best of everything, and every young man shall fall in love with you!"

Ellen felt her cheeks begin to glow. Her godmother would help her! She would dazzle Society at the balls, and be swept away by golden-haired Prince Christian!

"You will need to come to me, to prepare yourself and have your gowns fitted," her godmother said. "Pour the water back into the pitcher, so I can teach you the way to my home."

Carefully, Ellen tipped the broad basin back into the pitcher, then began pouring the water into the basin once more. It glowed green immediately, and her godmother gave her the directions to her palace.

She had suspected that her godmother was not merely some kindly sorceress, but also a woman of rank. And now it had been confirmed. Her godmother spoke with great elation at the prospect of Ellen coming at last to her palace, where the girl could be treated as befitted her birth. The only catch was that she would need to do it before midnight, but without being observed.

Ellen was about to ask if there was any other way, or if she shouldn't wait until everyone was asleep (which would be some time after midnight), when the sound of the latch turning made her jump and spill the rest of the water down her skirt.

Lydia, the maid who shared Ellen's room, put her hands on her hips in disgust. "Now I'll have to carry up another pitcher of water while you change," she groused.

"I'm sorry," Ellen whispered.

But it was no good. Lydia hated her. She had to make Ellen's bed every day, because Mrs. Hanks required the maids' rooms to be kept tidy at all times, and Ellen could never get the sheets to lie flat. Ellen could never remember to bring up two pitchers of water, one for her and one for Lydia, either. The one time she had remembered, she'd spilled both on her

way up the stairs, and had to mop up the spill and refill the pitchers. It was just like all of her other chores: no matter how hard she tried, she was useless.

And Ellen found that she was even more useless for the rest of the day. Thoughts of meeting her godmother in person, of setting foot in a palace where she wouldn't be expected to iron anything, filled her head. She tripped and tore the hem of her gown, spilled tea all over Poppy's coverlet, and dropped Marianne's freshly laundered handkerchiefs into a coal scuttle.

It was with great relief that Ellen found herself banished to the guest rooms to dust knickknacks with an ostrich plume. No one would look for her for hours, and she could always finish dusting after midnight, when she returned from her visit.

Besides, there were few valuable ornaments here and if she broke any, it would be no great loss. In fact, she rather thought that Lady Margaret might thank her for breaking one particular vase: it had a lopsided eagle painted on it, and one of the other maids had told Ellen that it would have been thrown out long ago if it hadn't been a gift from His Lordship's great-aunt.

As she hastily built a fire in the smallest and least-used guest room, Ellen kept her ears pricked for any sound from the corridor. The tinder wouldn't take, and in the end she threw her own handkerchief in to get things going. Building fires was another thing she could never do properly.

But at last she had a merry little blaze, which she promptly poured a glass of water over. Cringing, Ellen stuck her face into the smoke that roiled up and said, as instructed, "Cinders, cinders, smoke and water, take me to visit my dear godmother!"

The fireplace expanded, stretching like a waking cat until it was a tall doorway. Ellen scrambled to her feet and hiked her skirts high to step over the fender, into the mucky remains of her fire, and then on into the dark corridor beyond.

Her heart was hammering loudly in her throat, but more with excitement than fear. At the end of the corridor was a bright light, and she could hear music.

After eight years of neglect, she had finally found someone who wanted her.

Nightmare

Running down endless hallways carved of black stone, Poppy gasped and lifted her long trailing skirts higher. She couldn't remember how she got here, but she knew precisely where she was: the King Under Stone's palace of black rock and despair. Dressed in one of the bruise-colored Under Stone court gowns, she raced down corridor after corridor. None of the doors would open to her frantic tugging, but even if one of them did it wouldn't help her escape. There was only one door out of the Palace Under Stone, and she could not find it.

She turned a corner, and there before her was the silver gilt arch that led into the ballroom. The tall candles within were brightly lit, and she could hear shrill music and sharp laughter. She whirled around, wanting to avoid the attention of Under Stone and his sons, but the corridor behind her had closed off, and now there was nowhere else to go but forward.

She made herself breathe deeply, in and out, and compose her features. Perhaps they wouldn't notice she was here . . .

And then she corrected herself. The Under Stone she remembered was gone, killed by Galen with a silver knitting needle inscribed with the king's long-forgotten name. One of his sons was king now, and Poppy didn't know which one. That meant there were fewer princes to worry about as well. None of them had been as bright as their father, either, so it was very possible that she would escape detection.

She slipped into the ballroom and started to skirt around the edges of the floor. A tall and skeletally thin man grabbed her arms and swung her into the figures of a dance. She stumbled and would have fallen, but the other dancers pushed her back to her feet. They were laughing, their raucous voices slicing through her ears. They tossed her from partner to partner, their too-wide smiles and too-sharp teeth filling her vision.

"Stop!"

All eyes went to the dais.

Atop it a lean figure reclined on a black throne strewn with cushions that his father would have sneered at. The King Under Stone, who had once been Prince Rionin, looked down at Poppy with heavy-lidded eyes. He had been paired with Poppy's sister Jonquil, and was particularly cruel. Poppy's blood curdled at the thought of him possessing his father's power, and she hoped that Galen's chain was still holding the gate shut. But if it was, how had she gotten here?

Far more terrifying, at least from Poppy's point of view, was the young man standing to the left of the throne. It was her onetime suitor Blathen, and he was looking at Poppy as though she were a roast pheasant and he were starving.

"My dear brother pines for his lost bride," King Rionin said, putting a hand on Blathen's sleeve.

Poppy pulled the long hairpins out of her coiffure, and clutched one in each hand. "I'll kill you all first—I'll kill myself first!"

The figures on the dais just laughed at her.

"So dramatic," Blathen said, his voice caressing.

Turning her face away lest she be sick, Poppy saw the doorway that led out of the ballroom and to the entrance of the palace. She tried to get to it, but the courtiers blocked her way. She tripped and fell flat on the hard floor. The hairpins skittered out of her hands, and her hair tumbled over her face.

She clawed it away, frantic . . .

. . . and found herself sitting up in her bed in the Seadowns' manor.

Her heart was racing and her nightgown was plastered to her back with sweat, but she couldn't relax until she was certain that it had only been a dream. A nightmare, more like. She shoved aside the bedclothes and stumbled to the window, fumbling with the curtains to peer out the window.

There was the moon. She wasn't underground in that dark realm. She sagged against the windowsill, and her breath came out in sobs.

Poppy had nightmares quite frequently, but she had never shared them with anyone. She knew her family would find it alarming that tough, devil-may-care Poppy would still be haunted by the Midnight Balls. Only two of her sisters had

confessed to having nightmares about it: Pansy, who had been the most traumatized by their curse, and Orchid, who had been prone to night terrors anyway.

But this had not been like any other nightmare. Everything was so real: the feel of the gown, the floor under her feet, the music. Was it only because she was in a strange house, far from her family? Or was there something . . . wrong?

Putting on her dressing gown, Poppy went downstairs to make a cup of tea. She had just put her foot on the top stair when she heard a noise from farther down the corridor.

"Hello?" She was embarrassed to hear that her voice shook. "Who's there?"

There was a scuffling noise, and the sweat that still dampened the back of Poppy's nightgown froze. Stepping away from the stairs, she held her long nightgown away from her feet with one hand and carefully made a fist with the other, as Galen and Heinrich had taught her. She didn't want to break any fingers when she punched the intruder.

"I said, 'Hello?'" She was pleased that her voice was firmer now.

There was a faint cough, and then someone stepped into the light of one of the candles.

It was Ellen, and she was covered in black soot. Poppy stared at her in astonishment. Had she tried to sweep out one of the chimneys herself?

"What in heaven's name have you been doing?" Poppy only remembered to whisper at the last moment. They were just a few yards from the Seadowns' bedchamber.

"Nothing," Ellen said, but a mysterious smile crept onto her black-smeared face.

Poppy had had enough. First the nightmare, now Ellen wandering around in the night, shedding cinders on the carpets and acting as though she had some wonderful secret. The princess dragged Ellen down the hall into her room.

"Whatever do you think you're doing?" Poppy found it hard to berate the girl in a whisper, but she made do. "The Seadowns take you in, give you a job when no one else would, offer you gowns to attend the royal balls, and you—you—" She threw her hands in the air and then tried again. "You still break everything you touch, scorch the ironing—and why was there *sand* in my pillowcase last night? Is it *really* that hard to be a maid?" She stared at Ellen by the light of the candles she had lit in her room to chase away the shadows of the nightmare.

Ellen gazed down at the filthy toes of her shoes, peeping out from her sooty hem. When she at last looked at Poppy, instead of being ashamed or even sulky, her face was blazing with rage. Poppy took a step back in shock.

"Yes!" Ellen spat the word at Poppy. "Yes, it *is* that hard to be a maid, as you would know if you had ever lifted your little finger to do one simple thing for yourself, *Your Highness*." She sneered as she said the other girl's title. "Do you know how to make up a featherbed? To iron lace? To serve milady's tea just so?" Ellen was panting with the force of her emotions.

"N-no," Poppy stammered, still taken aback. "Well, I do know how to serve tea without breaking the—," she began, but Ellen interrupted her.

"And do you know what's it like to feel a tray of heirloom china leap from your hands and crash to the floor? To feel the iron suddenly go red hot even though it's not on the stove, and smell linen scorching? To find towels that you just folded in disarray even though no one has touched them? There is something horribly wrong with me. I wasn't meant to be a maid. And I just. Can't. Do it."

"You're not burning things on purpose?" This surprised Poppy as much as anything else Ellen had said. She and Marianne had assumed that Ellen was protesting her "fallen state" by wrecking the clothing and making the beds uncomfortable.

"Of course not!"

Tears started to spill from Ellen's eyes, and Poppy suppressed a groan. She never could stand to see anyone crying.

"Sometimes it's like something has taken over my body," Ellen sniffled. "I know what my hands should be doing, but I can't make them work right. Or I'll do something correctly, and then it undoes itself as soon as I turn my back." She shuddered. "It's a horrible feeling. I think my father's ill-luck cursed me."

Poppy knew that Ellen was probably speaking in the metaphorical sense, or at least being histrionic, but the words chilled her. *Cursed.* Poppy knew all about being cursed, at finding your body doing things you didn't want it to do. Like dance all night, even though your feet were bleeding inside your worn-out slippers.

She narrowed her eyes and studied the other girl. Perhaps Ellen was cursed, but why and by whom? Her life was already

in tatters, what good would it do to ruin her career as a maid-servant?

There were, of course, no outward signs that Ellen was cursed. What there was instead was a great deal of ash and soot drifting down on Poppy's carpet.

"But why are you so filthy? Did Mrs. Hanks tell you to clean out all the chimneys in the middle of the night?"

Ellen's tears dried as if by magic, and a sly, closed look came over her face. "Just trying to do my duty," she said stiffly. "If Your Highness will excuse me." It wasn't a question, and Ellen certainly didn't wait for an answer. She turned her back on Poppy and went out of the room.

Poppy flopped onto her bed. "Another mystery I'm not sure I want to solve," she muttered to herself.

Fencer

Dear Mother and Father,

Please help! I am being auctioned off to the highest bidder by King Rupert. Since I made it clear that I have no matrimonial interest in either Princess Hermione or Princess Emmeline, the king has determined that I will find a wife from among the Bretoner nobility. I am beginning to panic, and the holidays with their welcome return home are not for another month. What shall I do?

Your devoted son,
Christian

P.S. I have become good friends with the Westfalian princess, Poppy. She is tremendous fun, not at all the dangerous enchantress rumored. She does not dance (anymore) but is ruthless at cards. You would like her, Mother.

Christian sealed the letter and summoned a footman to post it. He thought about going himself, but he was hiding in his room. King Rupert had been quite frank about his reasons for throwing the balls and the fact that Christian was appalled had gone right over the Bretoner king's head. Princess Emmeline was in a snit that he hadn't chosen her, despite the obvious unsuitability of her young age, but seemed to agree with her father that Christian should at least marry a Bretoner lady, and right away.

He had tried to mollify them, to say that perhaps in a few years, when Emmeline was older, he might return and they would see if they suited. Although privately vowing to never set foot in Breton again just to avoid having to marry Emmeline, he had thought that this might help matters. But no, the king was insistent: he would see Christian betrothed by the holidays and there would be no argument.

Hoping that his parents truly weren't involved in Rupert's plan, Christian left the letter in the tray in the hallway for the butler to post. A bit behind schedule, he had to scramble to get dressed for the evening.

The Thwaites were having a dinner party to celebrate their oldest son's return from traveling the Far East. There was to be music and cards afterward, and Poppy was sure to be there with the Seadowns. Christian loved to watch Poppy win at cards.

~

Dickon Thwaite lunged and Christian easily stepped aside. A parry. A thrust. Another parry and Christian tapped Dickon's chest with the capped tip of his rapier.

"A hit!" The fencing master clapped his hands. "Very nice, Your Highness!"

Grimacing, Dickon shook his head when Christian offered another round. "You'll only win again," he said glumly. "Give Roger a good drubbing, why don't you?"

Christian wiped his face on the towel that a servant offered him, and turned to look inquiringly at the older Thwaite brother. It was the day after the Thwaites' dinner party, when Christian had found an instant rapport with the oldest brother, Roger. Taller and more sophisticated than his younger brother, Roger was already sighed after by a number of women, despite only being home a week.

"Shall we?" Christian flourished his rapier.

"With pleasure." Roger picked up his own weapon and came forward to the center of the floor, where the polished boards had been dusted with powdered resin to prevent the combatants from slipping. "But be warned: I have learned a few things in my travels."

"I like a challenge." Christian grinned, and lunged.

"Is that why you are courting Princess Poppy?" Roger easily parried and made conversation as though they sat at tea.

Christian nearly dropped his foil, and only just managed to skip out of the way of Roger's next attack. "Courting Poppy? We're friends," he said weakly. Sweat was pouring down his face, but that was from fencing. Of course.

"Ah."

"Roger has daring tastes in women as well," Dickon said

from the side of the room. "That's why he went to the Far East."

Roger looked irritated. "Actually, I went on the king's request, as part of the new ambassador's entourage," he said icily. He wasn't even slightly out of breath, while Christian thought he might have to forfeit before he collapsed.

"What was it really like?"

At dinner the night before, most of the conversation had been about the inconvenience of travel, and the general strangeness of foreigners, as viewed by Lady Thwaite's mother. Poppy and Christian were apparently not considered foreign, since they spoke Bretoner and wore clothes, which the elderly lady seemed to think foreign peoples eschewed.

"Fascinating," Roger said, and then he struck Christian, pressing the capped tip directly into the center of the Dane prince's sternum.

"A hit," the fencing master said, and clapped to end the bout. "Very nice, Lord Roger."

"Thank you." Roger handed his foil off to a servant, took a towel, and then turned back to Christian. "The Far East is steeped in magic in a way our side of the world hasn't been in centuries," he said. "When I returned and heard about Princess Poppy and her sisters, and the strange deaths that surrounded them a few years back, well, let me just say that I am not as prone to scoffing over such stories as some people are."

Still gripping his weapon, Christian felt his face harden. "What do you mean?" If Roger was insulting Poppy . . .

"I simply mean that if any more strange doings erupt around the Westfalian princesses, I recommend that you pay heed to even the most bizarre rumors about their past."

"Like Princess Rose stabbing someone with a darning needle?" Dickon had sidled over to eavesdrop, and now he laughed. "What kind of damage could that do?"

"From what I have heard," Roger said, giving his brother a quelling look, "Rose's husband, Galen, used a knitting needle to kill a creature that was nothing that I should like to face."

Christian wanted to know more, much more, without it seeming that his interest was as a prospective suitor. Fortunately, he had already accepted an invitation from Dickon for tea at the Thwaites' manor after their fencing excursion.

He had decided to accept any and all invitations he received in order to get as far from Tuckington Palace as possible. Princess Emmeline had decided quite abruptly that morning that she was heartbroken over Christian, and was trailing about the palace in a drab gown with her hair in a tangle, sighing and dabbing her eyes with a handkerchief until she made the skin around them quite red. Christian suspected it had more to do with the Analousian novel he had seen her reading the day before than any fondness for him personally. In addition to that, King Rupert kept popping out of his study at random times to bark questions at Christian, demanding to know whether the prince preferred plump or slim women, dark or fair.

It was all too uncomfortable for words, and Christian counted himself lucky to have found so many friends so

quickly in Breton. He was always welcome at the Thwaites or Seadowns, and other invitations came often. Of course, the latter came from households with eligible young ladies, but anything was better than the palace.

It was quite easy to ply Roger for information about the Westfalian princesses over tea. Although not someone who enjoyed gossiping, Roger clearly believed this to be more a matter of sharing possibly vital knowledge. Most of what he knew was hardly a secret, however. The princesses had worn out their dancing shoes in some mysterious fashion nearly every night, and the princes who tried to uncover their secret died afterward, but never on Westfalian soil.

What Christian and Dickon had never heard before, though, was that a dark sorcerer had been involved, and that Rose's husband Galen had been working with some benevolent magicians to end the princesses' curse.

"How do you know this?" Christian stirred his tea but didn't drink, too engrossed—almost sickened—by the story.

"An herbalist from the Silk Road region of the East was with the ambassador for a time, just before I came home. His Lordship suffers terribly from the headache," Roger explained. He added sugar to his tea and sipped it in his elegant way. Really, he was one of the most self-contained, even graceful, men that Christian had ever seen. "Lon Qui knew the white magicians who aided this Galen Werner."

"What did you say about Galen?"

The parlor door had just opened, and Poppy and Marianne stood there. Marianne's mouth was open in surprise, but Poppy

looked murderous. She clutched at her reticule as though it contained a weapon. Realizing that it probably held some very sharp knitting needles, Christian reflected that it did.

"Ah, Your Highness!" Roger actually seemed nonplussed. He got to his feet hastily, his napkin falling from his knee to the floor. Christian and Dickon rose as well, but all they could do was stand there looking guilty.

"What did you just say about Galen?" Poppy demanded an answer when none of the gentlemen would offer one.

"We were merely, ah, talking," Roger said evasively.

"I am well aware of that, and you seem to be talking about my family." Poppy's voice was icy.

"Roger was just telling us that there was magic involved, when your brother-in-law . . . the slippers . . . and all that," Christian babbled. There was something in Poppy's face. She wasn't angry . . . she looked hurt. There was a great deal of gossip about her family, and he imagined that it never got any easier to walk into a room and find that you were the topic of discussion.

"And what does Roger know about it?"

"I am acquainted with an Eastern herbalist, Your Highness, who knew the magicians who assisted your brother-in-law." It didn't take long for Roger to regain his composure; Christian had to give him that.

"How nice for you," Poppy snapped. "Marianne? I'm leaving; do you wish to stay?"

"No," Marianne said. She flashed a confused look at

Dickon, who could only open and close his mouth like a fish. "Good day, gentlemen."

Before Christian or his companions could react, Poppy and Marianne were gone again, a footman trailing in their wake and looking as embarrassed as Christian and the Thwaite brothers.

Gown

I've changed my mind," Poppy said.

"What, again?" Lady Margaret's voice was amused and calm.

She was always calm. Poppy had to admit that she found herself behaving better in the face of Her Ladyship's sublime tranquility. Even now, refusing to go to the ball she had tentatively agreed to attend, Poppy was trying for serenity rather than fleeing the room and hiding.

"Just wait a moment before you decide," Lady Margaret said. "Wait until you see your new gown."

Taking Poppy by the hand, Lady Margaret led her over to the windows, where a dress form had been draped with a thin sheet of muslin. Letting go of Poppy's hand, Lady Margaret took hold of the sheet and drew it aside with a grand flourish.

Much to her embarrassment, Poppy had a completely

girlish reaction: she gasped, and even clapped her hands. Then she blushed and would have fled, but the dress was too magnificent and she had to inspect it from every angle.

The dressmaker had agreed that white would be too plain for the pale-skinned princess. So the gown of heavy white silk was trimmed with poppy red, and her namesake flower was embroidered randomly across the skirt. It was gorgeous and daring and everything Poppy could want in a ball gown.

The only drawback was that if she wanted anyone to see her in it, she would have to attend a ball. Imagining Christian's face when she walked into Tuckington Palace in that gown would be worth it, however.

"Christian *has* to see you in this," Marianne said breathily, echoing Poppy's thought.

Ducking her head so they couldn't see her face, Poppy fingered the neckline of the dress. It was low, and the red silk trim was wide and luxurious.

"It is a very fine gown," Poppy admitted. "Thank you, Cousin Margaret."

"You are quite welcome, my dear," Lady Margaret said, a knowing look on her face. "Does the prospect of wearing it entice you to attend at least the royal gala?"

"It does," Poppy agreed graciously.

"And that whatever it is you've been knitting is the same color," Marianne pointed out.

"It's a stole," Poppy reminded her.

She had, fortuitously, been knitting herself a stole out of

a fine yarn the exact color of these poppies. It would look stunning hanging from her elbows over the skirt of this gown. Everyone always told her that shades of violet and blue were her best colors, but Poppy had a certain fondness for red that she never got to indulge quite enough.

Which, of course, Lady Margaret had figured out.

"And don't worry about dancing," Lady Margaret told her. "At a gala like this one, there will be a great deal to keep you occupied. No cards, but food and music and fireworks. Acrobats and fire-eaters in the garden as well."

Marianne twirled around in delight. "And scientific displays of strange machines, and poetry readings, and all kinds of things. When King Rupert hosts a gala, he spares no expense."

"Apparently," Poppy said.

She wondered, briefly, what it would have been like to be a princess growing up in the massive Tuckington Palace, with fire-eaters and gala balls. She herself had had to share a bedchamber and also a maid with two of her sisters. And until very recently, when Westfalin's economy finally took a turn for the better, she had only gotten new gowns for very special occasions like Rose's and Lily's weddings. After all, she had four older sisters to pass on their wardrobes.

Someone tapped at the door and came in. It was Ellen, and she had a pile of freshly washed and ironed linens. At least they probably had been freshly washed and ironed at some point, but now Poppy could see at least one scorch mark and something like fine soot dusted across on the white cloth. She sighed. Ellen always had soot on her these days, and would

never say why. There was a streak of it on her forehead right now. Since their confrontation last week, Ellen had refused to even make eye contact with the princess, and her household skills had degenerated even further.

"Why are there cinders on Poppy's shifts?" Marianne blew across the pile as Ellen set her basket on a chair.

Another sigh, this one from Ellen.

Lady Margaret put a restraining hand on her daughter's arm. "Ellen," she said kindly, "did you still want to go to the royal balls?"

"Yes, Your Ladyship," Ellen said demurely, but Poppy could swear she saw a secretive look in the girl's eyes.

"There is still time for me to have Monsieur Delatour make a gown for you," Lady Margaret said. "Or you are much of a size with Poppy and Marianne. We could retrim one of theirs . . ." Her voice trailed off as the young maid shook her head vehemently, shedding more black powder onto Poppy's clothes and the floor.

"No, thank you, my lady. I have a patroness who has provided me with gowns." Ellen's voice was wooden, and Poppy's eyes narrowed.

The other girl was hiding something: glee, disdain, some other emotion. And why? If there was someone willing to help her, why shouldn't she let the Seadowns know?

Lady Margaret had the same question.

"How lovely, my dear! Who is it?"

"She wishes to remain anonymous," Ellen said silkily. And then she turned and flounced out of the room.

Marianne rolled her eyes, but Poppy didn't smile. Something was going on with Ellen, something beyond bad manners and worse domestic skills.

"If you two will excuse me," Poppy said, with far more grace than Ellen would ever be able to muster. "I really must write to my sisters." And Galen, she added mentally.

"To tell them about the gown, and how you're going to the royal gala with us?" Marianne raised one eyebrow.

"Yes, yes," Poppy lied. Though she might actually mention her beautiful new gown, she had other things to write about. Like asking if Galen knew of any spells that left a residue of soot.

"And wait until you see the costume I picked for the masked ball," Marianne said as she and her mother left the room. "You have to come!"

"We shall see," Poppy promised, giving her friend a small smile as she shut the door.

Secretly Poppy knew that she would never go to the masked ball. Nothing could be more horrible than being surrounded by strange people garbed in even stranger masks, their hard eyes staring out from hideous, inhuman faces . . .

She shuddered, and hurried to the writing desk. Galen might know something, and if not, perhaps he could find out for her.

Preparations

Ellen lounged in the enormous bathtub, giggling with pleasure. Made of glass blown in the shape of a flower, it was easily the size of a small pool, with a padded bench so the bather's head didn't sink below the surface. She leaned against the back of the tub, perfectly curved to fit her shoulders, and inhaled deeply the scent of roses and precious oils.

She could feel all the dirt and degradation of servitude sliding away into the swirling water. It was glorious, and she never wanted it to end.

Tonight was the night of the royal gala, and she was in her godmother's palace, preparing for her grand debut. She'd fabricated an errand, saying that Princess Poppy needed ribbons for her hair, to leave Seadown House. Then she snuck back in one of the side doors and ran to a guest room to build a fire and make her escape into her godmother's realm.

A maidservant in green held out a towel the size of a bed sheet. Ellen stretched with languid grace and got out of the bath. The maid wrapped her in the towel and helped Ellen lie on a padded table. The maid began to vigorously rub her charge with the towel, then with oils and lotions. The unguents smelled so heavenly that Ellen drifted away into a wondrous dream.

In the dream she was dancing with a handsome prince on a cloud that smelled of primroses. The prince had dark hair and was so tall that the top of her head only came to the middle of his chest. Ellen frowned a little, and made the prince shorter and golden-haired, like Prince Christian. The maid rubbed her forehead to get rid of the frown lines, and once more the prince turned dark and impossingly tall. He reminded her of someone . . .

Ellen's eyes snapped open, and another maid was hovering over her head. This one was combing out the girl's long dark hair with a golden comb, while the other was now busy smearing something that tingled over Ellen's feet. The maid moved on to a different lotion for Ellen's calves, but the girl's feet still tingled.

"I don't believe I like that foot lotion," Ellen said, closing her eyes again.

The maid didn't answer. But then, none of her godmother's servants ever spoke. It was odd, and a bit distressing, but they appeared to all be mute. However, even the eerie, silent servants could hardly detract from the glorious golden walls, the shining sapphire floors, the blown glass columns, and the rest of the ornaments of the Corley's palace.

When a voice finally did answer her, Ellen jumped.

"That lotion is a special treatment for your feet," said her godmother. "So you can dance all night!"

Her godmother laughed, and Ellen joined in.

Draped in a shimmering silk dressing robe as light as gauze, Ellen followed her godmother into a room filled with gorgeous gowns. She had been there before; these rooms were hers whenever she visited her godmother. She had tried on many of the dresses, putting on one after another and admiring herself in the long mirrors. Silent seamstresses took her measurements and made sure that each bodice fitted as if had been pasted on, each skirt was just the right length, no sleeve was too binding or too loose.

Ellen knew exactly which gown she wanted to wear this evening. It was exactly the sort of thing she had dreamed of these past horrible years since her parents' deaths. Sea colored, it seemed to float whenever she took it down to admire it.

"No, no," her godmother said as Eleanora reached for the gown now. "Not that old thing. You must have something very special for tonight. But first . . ."

She clapped her plump hands, which made a surprisingly sharp noise, and servants came running in. They took Ellen's dressing gown and put her in underclothes so white and fine that it was almost a shame to cover them. Then a corset, laced so tight she could hardly breathe, and after that layer after layer of petticoats, embroidered with tiny scarlet roses.

And then the gown. The magnificent gown.

It was so heavy that it took two women to carry it. Luxurious

white silk nearly as thick as velvet, lined with scarlet, embroidered heavily with scarlet roses and encrusted with rubies and pearls at the neckline. There were no laces or hooks: when they had it over Eleanora's head a seamstress sewed up the back seam of the gown.

It fit like her own skin, and yet was so heavy and dramatic that she knew she could never not be aware of it. She looked in the mirrors and tears began to drip down her cheeks.

"It is so beautiful!"

"And you deserve it, my lovely," her godmother said. The woman was looking her up and down with satisfaction, almost greed. "You deserve it."

Her godmother clapped her hands again, and more servants entered. They sat Ellen carefully on a low stool, with her skirts spread out around her, and expertly applied cosmetics to her face. Then her long hair was brushed through with a shining pomade and twisted up into an elaborate coiffure.

After that, to Ellen's rapturous delight, jewels were brought in. A choker of rubies, ruby and diamond pins for her hair, a ring and bracelet. The servants placed them reverently upon her, and she was ready for the ball, with the exception of her feet.

"Oh, what about slippers?" As she had stood to admire herself in the mirrors again, Ellen felt the slick floor beneath her bare soles and realized that she wasn't even wearing stockings or garters beneath her gown, let alone shoes.

"This way, my darling girl," her godmother said, and took her arm with one soft hand.

"I have such special slippers for you that you will not need stockings," the smiling old woman continued as they went down a long corridor lined with flowers made of glass. "They would only spoil the effect."

The cold glass floor chilled Ellen's feet. She couldn't fathom going out in public without stockings—she would be half-naked! What if she lifted her skirts too high and exposed her bare legs to the royal court?

Her godmother read the girl's alarm easily and chuckled. "Now, now! Have I not provided for everything else? These are very special shoes, as I've said. They will help you to dance like a dream! No one will notice that you aren't wearing stockings, even if they do catch a glimpse of your ankles. Don't you trust me?"

Not wanting to seem ungrateful to the kind lady who had given her so much, Ellen pushed aside her fears and smiled back. She went with her godmother into a circular room she had never seen before, and let a servant help her into a large chair with a footstool. Both chair and footstool, like so much of this glorious palace, were made of delicate glass that was as hard as steel. She sat rigidly, not wanting to crease her gown or muss her hair on the tall back of the chair, and her godmother bustled over to a long table where there were strange instruments and bubbling pots set over weird green flames in golden pans.

Goose bumps broke out all over Ellen, and she felt sweat starting on her temples. She gritted her teeth, not wanting the powder on her face to run. But here was magic, magic beyond walking through a fireplace into a palace.

And it was going to be practiced on her.

She looked down at her gown, at the rubies on her wrist and finger, and straightened her spine. It would be worth it, to dance in this gown, these jewels. To win a prince's love and leave drudgery far behind.

And besides, her godmother would never hurt her.

Honored Guest

Welcome, all, to the first night of our royal gala!"

King Rupert stood atop a dais that had been erected in the Tuckington Palace gardens. The dais was cleverly positioned at the edge of a large pond, and the water helped carry his voice to the assembled crowd, who cheered.

"We hope you will all enjoy yourselves while you get to know our most honored guest, Prince Christian of the Danelaw!"

Another huge cheer and Christian sheepishly took his place beside the king. He gave the crowd a small wave, feeling self-conscious, and looked for a friendly face. Thank heavens tonight wasn't the masked ball: he was still preparing himself for that. In his experience, masked balls were rife with opportunities for people to do and say things they wouldn't normally, and for good reason.

A gown of white and red at the front of the crowd caught his eye. White and red, worn by a young woman with black hair and milky white skin. It was Poppy, naturally. No other young lady would be so daringly dressed. Beside her was Marianne, looking demure but lovely in green. He couldn't quite tell, but it seemed that Poppy was either smirking, or at the least smiling, at his discomfort. He decided to use his "guest of honor" prerogative to steal a dance with her.

"Let the gala begin!" King Rupert raised his hands grandly, and fireworks erupted from each side of the dais.

There was more cheering, and then Christian could make his escape. Or so he thought. The king at once handed him off to the queen, and Christian found himself leading Her Majesty into the palace ballroom to open the dancing. As he moved in stately circles around the room, Queen Edith twittered in his ear about this lady and that lady, making sure that he knew exactly whom his hosts expected him to dance with. He wondered if he would even have time to eat something, let alone persuade Poppy to dance just this once.

And he wanted to squire Marianne as well. She was not only a delightful dancer, but he enjoyed teasing her. He knew that there were some rumors about his fondness for the Seadowns' daughter, but he thought of her as one of his own sisters, and was hoping to be invited to her wedding before the year was out.

At last his dance with the queen ended, and as he bowed he caught a glimpse of scarlet and white in the doorway of the ballroom. He gave another flourish, and turned toward the flash of color, saying, "My next partner, I think."

But when he faced the young lady who had just entered, it was not Poppy at all.

He had thought that only one person would possibly wear such a dramatic gown, or have that gleaming black hair, but it seemed there were two. This young lady was beautiful and her coloring was similar to Poppy's, but her hair wasn't as black and her eyes were more blue than violet. Close up, he never would have mistaken the two girls.

But now here he was, facing this lady who looked slightly familiar and was smiling at him in an expectant way. The entire room had paused, staring, and he gallantly held out his hand.

"Would you care to have this dance?"

"Thank you, Your Highness." Her voice was light and caressing, and again very familiar. It taunted him, and he racked his brain for her identity. He had met so many young ladies during his stay in Breton, but surely he would remember one this beautiful, and with such striking coloring. She wasn't a Casterton, and definitely not a Richmond. A Blythe?

There really had been far too many prospective brides paraded before him. They couldn't possibly expect him to know all their names. He swallowed his pride as the figures of the dance moved them closer together.

"I'm quite sorry, but I seem to have forgotten your name."

"That's because we were never formally introduced." She gave a light tinkle of laughter. "My name is Lady El—Lady Ella."

"Lady Ella . . . ?" He waited, but no family name was forthcoming.

"We've only seen each other in passing, it would hardly have been memorable."

"Ah."

Their conversation continued in this stilted fashion for the rest of the dance. Christian tried a few sallies: where had they met? Did he know her parents? But she replied only with mysterious smiles and increasingly forced laughter, even though none of his attempts were all that funny.

It was with great relief that he bowed to her at the end of the dance. She reached for his hand again, rather boldly, to encourage another dance, but another gentleman came up just then.

It was Roger Thwaite, and he was staring at Lady Ella with an expression of shock. "Eleanora?"

Lady Ella bubbled with laughter, but it sounded even more strained than her previous giggles. "Oh my! It seems that no one can remember my name this evening!" She tapped Roger's arm with her folded fan, and then Christian's for good measure.

Christian barely stopped himself from rubbing the spot where her ivory-and-silk fan had struck him, and hoped that she'd been a little gentler with Roger. Really, the girl was quite strange, stranger than Poppy even.

"I don't know who this Eleanora is," she babbled. "I'm Lady Ella."

"Sorry." Roger drew himself up, embarrassed. "For a moment I mistook you for an old friend." He gallantly held out his hand. "Please say you will honor me with this next dance, so I may make up for my mistake?"

Lady Ella looked at Christian, who was tongue-tied. Roger

clearly wanted to dance with this odd young woman, and Christian wanted to find Poppy, but Ella seemed to have set her cap for the prince.

The awkward moment was saved by a small hand being laid on Christian's forearm, just where Lady Ella had slapped him with her fan. He looked down to see Marianne smiling up at him.

"I believe you promised *me* this dance," she said, smiling.

"Ah, Marianne, sorry to make you wait," Christian replied with relief, and whirled her away.

The dance had already begun, but it was a reel and anyone could join in. On the other hand, it was so fast that there was no way for them to talk. Christian wanted to ask where Poppy was, and Marianne kept questioning him about Lady Ella. In the end they excused themselves before the dance was finished, and went to one of the refreshment rooms to talk and drink lemonade.

"Where's Poppy?"

"Watching the jugglers in the gardens," Marianne said. "I came in to dance, and saw that girl and her gown." Her cheerful expression darkened. "Mama will be so put out! She specially wanted Poppy and I to have unique dresses, but it looks like someone bribed our dressmaker to copy one of them. Who was she?"

"She said her name was Lady Ella, but she wouldn't give me a family name. She looked familiar, and told me that we'd met in passing, but I just can't remember where."

"Ella?" Marianne's brow creased. "Ella who?"

"Are you certain you don't know her?" Christian simply could not put his finger on it, but there was something about Lady Ella that nagged him.

Carrying her glass in one hand and resting the other on Christian's arm, Marianne steered them both back to the ballroom. She scanned the dancers until she spotted the lavish white and scarlet gown, watching the girl who wore it with narrowed eyes. Then she drank half her lemonade in one gulp.

"I don't know her," she hissed. "But someone here must! She's wearing more jewels than the queen, and Society is not that large."

"She claims that she and I did meet," Christian said. "But we weren't properly introduced." He blinked eyes a few times. His vision was filled with scarlet roses on white, swirling beneath the glittering lights. Lady Ella's shoes flashed like rubies.

"Very odd," Marianne agreed. "But why did she have to ruin Poppy's dress by copying it? What is her game?"

"Game?" Christian felt incredibly thick. Couldn't they just stand and watch the girl in the scarlet shoes twirling around and around? Why did Marianne have to talk so viciously about poor Lady Ella?

"Yes, what's going on?" said a voice behind them. "Someone told me I absolutely had to come in and view the dancing."

Christian turned to find Poppy standing there looking puzzled. Unconsciously he reached for the silk watch fob that Poppy had knitted for him, hoping she would notice that he

was wearing it. The muzziness in his head cleared, and he could see that her dress was different from Ella's. The red was more subdued, and the flowers on the skirt were poppies, naturally, not roses. She also had a long red shawl draped around her arms, and her hair was thicker, her eyes larger. He couldn't believe that he'd mistaken anyone else for her.

"Look over there. Dancing with Roger Thwaite!" Marianne grabbed Poppy by the shoulders and turned her.

Still looking puzzled, Poppy looked out into the dancers for a moment, and tilted her head to one side. "Who is . . . I can't quite see . . ."

"What do you mean? She's right there!" Marianned pointed again.

Christian gave her an irritated look. She was disturbing his reverie. The red roses on white silk whirled by again.

Poppy muttered something, and then gasped in shock. "It can't be her!"

"You recognize her?" Marianne stared. "Where did you meet her? She introduced herself to Christian as Lady Ella, no last name." She wrinkled her nose.

"Interesting," Poppy said slowly. "I guess she did find a patron, but did she have to upstage my gown?" Poppy made a face.

Christian fought down a sudden urge to shake Poppy. Wouldn't someone tell him more about the fascinating Lady Ella? He brought himself up short with that thought, and took a drink of his lemonade. He felt very strange.

"Not just that," Marianne said, and Christian realized that the two girls had more or less forgotten his presence. "But she's dripping with jewels! Why do I not know who she is?"

This brought Poppy's attention fully away from Lady Ella and onto Marianne. "You don't recognize her at all?"

"No! Who is she?" Marianne shifted uneasily. "And why is everyone staring at us?"

"Why wouldn't they stare?" Poppy said. "They want to know what I think of that gown!"

Christian threw up his hands. "Will someone please at least tell me why this girl shouldn't have a gown and jewels?"

Poppy patted his shoulder but her eyes were still on Lady Ella, as were the eyes of everyone there. "Sorry. It's just that . . . this girl . . . has no money. So how did she come by the gown and jewels? It's troubling." Poppy was running the edges of her stole through her fingers, staring at Lady Ella.

Christian didn't care who Lady Ella's patron was. He only knew that she was beautiful, and danced like a fairy creature. He wondered if Roger would mind Christian cutting in, even though the dance wasn't finished.

"Now, now, Your Highness!" A voice behind them boomed and someone clapped Christian on the back so hard that he nearly fell on his face. "No stealing all the young ladies!"

A large, florid man—Duke Something-or-other—was looking over both Poppy and Marianne with a roguish eye. "You're supposed to be looking for a nice Bretoner wife," he announced, blasting whiskey-scented breath at Christian. "So I'll take this one off your hands!"

Without waiting to see if Christian protested or if Poppy agreed, the duke took hold of Poppy and spun her out onto the dance floor.

"Poppy doesn't dance, everyone knows that," Marianne said, bristling with indignation now that the initial shock was over.

Christian fought down a surge of jealousy. He'd been planning on convincing Poppy to dance with him—just once! And now this drunken duke had taken her off against her will. She would probably never dance again after this.

It was clear that Poppy was trying to get free of her partner's overzealous grip. Every time the dance called for a turn or spin Poppy tried to slip away, but the duke kept hauling her back to his side. It would have been comical but for two things: Poppy was such a skilled dancer that she made it look like part of the dance, and the expression of outrage on her face made it clear she was not attempting to be funny.

"What an odd person this Princess Poppy is," said Lady Ella, tripping up to Christian with Roger Thwaite in tow. "I can assure you, Your Highness, that I love dancing. Shall we?" Once more she held out her hand for Christian to dance with her.

Christian found himself reaching to take her hand without thinking about it. At the last second he remembered his manners and stopped to look inquiringly at Roger.

"I would like to speak with Lady Marianne," Roger said in a stiff voice.

"If I'm not imposing, then," Christian murmured, and took Ella's outstretched hand.

Christian did his best, as they danced, to not be distracted by Poppy's situation. Ella was a good dancer, and she seemed more relaxed now. The smell of her perfume made him want to bury his face in her hair, and he concentrated on Poppy to avoid making an idiot of himself over the beauteous Lady Ella.

His partner, for her part, kept shooting the odd glance back at Roger and Marianne, who were deep in conversation on the opposite side of the room.

Christian wondered if it would be rude to ask her outright where she had gotten her gown, and why she had copied Poppy's, but he simply couldn't bring himself to do it. So he laughed heartily at the mysterious Lady Ella's forced jokes, and led her through the measures of the dance.

Dance

Poppy could not believe that she was dancing for the first time in three years, and it was with this . . . this . . .

No epithet was strong enough to describe this horrible drunken clod, in her opinion. Adding insult to injury was the fact that he was such a terrible dancer.

She contemplated faking a faint, or a sprained ankle, but didn't want her boorish partner to turn heroic and try to carry her off somewhere. Hearing the titters of the other dancers who noticed her trying to slip away, she forced herself to relax. It was just one dance, and then she would hurry to the gardens before anyone else could try and pull her back onto the dance floor.

A flash of scarlet and white made her turn her head, and she saw Christian dancing by with Ellen. She forgot about her partner—the dance was an Analousian pavane, something she had been able to do in her sleep since the age of eight—and turned her mind back to the Ellen situation.

She didn't for a moment think that Ellen had found some wealthy Society patron. No, she had gotten herself caught up in some sort of an enchantment, which Poppy considered far worse. No wonder Marianne couldn't recognize her own maid: just trying to look at Ellen had made Poppy's eyes blur, and she was wearing protective talismans. It wasn't until she had said a rhyme that Galen had taught her that she had been able to see Ellen clearly.

Now Ellen's soot-covered ramblings through Seadown House were explained, but not entirely. Who or what was helping Ellen? Nothing human could have made a gown that elaborate in less than two days, and no one but the dressmaker and his assistants had seen Poppy's gown before it was delivered.

And that was when Poppy began to worry. The jewels that Ellen wore gleamed in a way that was almost taunting, and so did her gown. Ellen dipped and spun as the princess watched her, and Poppy caught a glimpse of her dancing slippers.

They looked to be made out red glass, but Poppy clearly saw them bend with Ellen's foot. The sight of them seared her eyes, and she almost had to veil her gaze with her shawl to clear her vision.

"Quite stolen your thunder, hasn't she?" Poppy's partner practically shouted in her ear. "You're pretty enough, no need to scratch her eyes out!"

"Excuse me?" Poppy gave him a cold look.

"Have to ask her for a dance myself," her partner went on, oblivious. "Quite the looker, quite the looker."

Poppy stared at him in disbelief. This really went beyond

boorish, she thought. Good manners dictated that a man not admire another woman in front of his current dance partner. And his voice had been loud enough for half the room to hear!

"Why don't you ask her to dance right now?" Poppy snapped.

She finally freed herself from the duke's grasp and stalked off the dance floor. She looked over her shoulder just once, briefly, and saw her partner doing just as she had suggested—walking straight through the rest of the dancers on his way to Ellen without so much as a glance back at Poppy.

Her faced burned, and she peeked at the bystanders nearest her to see who else was witnessing her shame. But no one was even looking in her direction. They were all fixated on Ellen, Christian, and the duke as he attempted to interrupt the dance and take Ellen's hand away from the prince.

To Poppy's great satisfaction, Christian handed over Ellen with only a moment of reluctance. Then he immediately sought out Poppy. He had a bemused look on his face, however.

"An unusual girl," he muttered as he reached Poppy's side.

"Very," Poppy said curtly, and straightened Christian's jacket for him. She saw that he was wearing the watch ribbon she had knit for him, and she warmed slightly. "I don't want to tell tales, if she wants to be incognito, but I will venture that she's done something she's going to regret to get that gown."

"If you're going to keep dropping mysterious hints . . . ," Christian said with a warning in his voice.

"You'll do what?" Poppy asked archly. Then she made a

face. “But truly,” she said hesitantly. “I’m worried. I have . . . experience with what happens when you make bargains you shouldn’t . . . in order to get what you want.”

“Even more mysterious,” Christian said.

“Well, I—” Poppy hesitated again, uncertain.

If she told Christian the details of her family’s story, what would he say? And would it help matters? The more she watched Ellen in her fabulous gown, covered with a queen’s ransom in jewels, the more she was certain that something was about to go terribly wrong.

“There’s something you should know. I—that is, my mother—,” Poppy began, but Christian stopped her.

“Here comes Marianne, Roger, Dickon, and Lady Margaret.” He pointed over her shoulder. “And Marianne looks to be in deep dudgeon, as the Bretoners say.”

Poppy turned and saw that it was true. Dickon and Lady Margaret just looked confused, but Marianne was indeed in deep dudgeon while Roger Thwaite’s handsome face was creased with concern. Poppy sighed, half with relief and half with regret. She wasn’t about to spill the story of her mother’s mistake in front of such an audience, which felt simultaneously like a reprieve and a disappointment.

“Please promise you’ll continue your story later,” Christian said in an undertone as they were joined by their friends.

“We’ll see,” Poppy said.

“Poppy knows who she is,” Marianne was saying. “Don’t you, Poppy?”

Lady Margaret squinted at the drunken duke and his mesmerizing dance partner. "But Marianne, I don't know what you're talking about," she said. "I would recognize anyone Poppy had been introduced to, and I have no idea who that young woman is. I'm quite put out that she managed to copy Poppy's gown, but other than that . . . Will you look at those slippers? How breathtaking!"

Lady Margaret applauded with the rest of the company as the dance came to an end and Ellen breathlessly curtsied to her partner. Already the girl's eyes were searching the crowd for Christian. But, Poppy noticed, they stopped for a moment on Roger Thwaite before skipping on to the prince. Roger, for his part, couldn't take his gaze from Ellen. But rather than the avid expression that everyone else in the room seemed to be giving her, he had a look of mixed longing and unease.

"Roger," Poppy said quietly, putting a hand on his arm. "Do you know her?"

The older Thwaite brother looked down at her, his brows knit tightly together. "Yes," he said simply. "Do you?"

Poppy drew him aside before saying, "She's our maid. But Marianne and Lady Margaret don't recognize her—I almost didn't myself. Something is very wrong here."

"Your *maid*?" Roger's mouth turned down even farther. "Poor Eleanora!" His eyes sought out the girl whose hand had just been claimed by another partner before she could reach her clear goal: Christian. "I had no idea . . . after her mother's death she just disappeared!"

"You knew her before?" Poppy stared at Roger, and watched him swallow as his eyes followed Ellen around the room.

"We were very close as children," he said after a long pause.

Feeling awkward, Poppy clenched her fists in the edges of her stole. Clearly Roger still cared for his childhood friend. And, just as clearly, whatever glamour Ellen had placed over the rest of the assembly did not extend to him.

She wondered what resistence to magic Roger had, that he could see her clearly. Poppy had been so nervous about attending the royal gala—not that she would have ever let anyone know—that she had taken extra precautions. Rather than her usual silk garters, she had fastened her stockings with garters she had made from virgin wool. They had been knit with silver needles that had been blessed by her family's bishop, and then she had boiled the garters with nightshade and basil. They itched terribly but she hoped they would protect her from harm and permit her to see through any enchantments. And they had.

"How is it you recognized her?" Roger had torn his eyes from Ellen.

"I'm wearing protective . . . garments," Poppy said. She had been on the verge of saying "garters," and it was a measure of how much propriety she had learned from Lady Margaret that she bit her tongue just in time.

"I was given one by a Far Eastern magician," Roger said gravely. He patted the breast of his shirt, and Poppy could vaguely see the outline of a small lump there. "A bone from

some strange beast that has been rubbed with sacred oils and hung on a raw silk cord."

"I should like to see that sometime," Poppy said, thinking that it sounded much more comfortable than her own protective talismans. "But we really must find out where Ellen—Eleanora, that is—got her gown.

"You know somewhat of my family's curse," she went on, fighting back her still fresh hurt over finding Christian, Dickon, and Roger gossiping about her over tea. "So you know how making a deal with a magical being can turn on you."

"Indeed," Roger said. "But perhaps here is not the place. I don't think Eleanora will answer any of our questions, at least not tonight. She pretended not to know me, and looked most distressed when I questioned her. I do not think that she is under magical constraint not to answer, merely that she prefers to be Lady Ella here and now."

"Let's hope so," Poppy said fervently. "I for one would like to ask her some questions, and get some straight responses out of her."

Roger looked surprised, and Poppy gave a tight laugh. "Let me guess: your friend Eleanora was so sweet-natured, and would never have hidden a secret from you?" She didn't even wait for his confirming nod. "Well, *Ellen* is of a different temperament." But then Poppy did pause, remembering her own ordeal, and grimaced. She didn't exactly feel pity toward Ellen-Eleanora, but she felt more charitable. "Or it may just be too painful for her to speak to you."

"But why? She seems to speak to Christian freely enough." Once more, Roger looked toward the girl who was again dancing with the prince in her gown of red roses on white silk.

Poppy, too, was looking at them. Her hands were clenched so hard in the edges of her stole that the silk squeaked. Christian was looking down at "Lady Ella" with a dazed expression.

"That, as you Bretoners say, is part and parcel of what we need to discover," Poppy said.

Midnight

When the enormous clock at the far end of the ballroom struck half past eleven, Ellen felt a wave of relief wash over her. She hadn't thought it would be so: the gala would last until dawn, and hearing that her godmother expected her to be home by midnight had been a disappointment.

But then the glass had been melted onto her feet.

Despite the tingling lotion that her godmother's maid had slathered over them, the heat of the molten glass had been shocking. Just the sight of that glowing, smoking stuff coating her white skin had made her dizzy.

"Courage," her godmother had said, a broad smile on her plump face. "Courage." And with delicate golden instruments her godmother had shaped the glass into an elaborate pair of high-heeled dancing slippers.

"You must return to me by midnight," her godmother had told her. "My power in the outside world fades once night begins the turn toward dawn."

And so as soon as the Bretoner reel she had been dancing with Prince Christian ended, Ellen curtsied to the prince and bid him good evening. It was quarter to twelve now, but if she hurried she wouldn't be too late.

"But wait—why?" Prince Christian reached out to reclaim her hands. As the evening had worn on, he had become more and more enthralled by her.

A pleased thrill ran through Ellen, and she hoped that people were watching. Rather than grinning in triumph, as she would have liked to, she kept to her godmother's advice to remain aloof and mysterious.

"I must go," she said, trying to make her voice light and caressing. "But perhaps there will be another ball, and another opportunity to dance . . ." She slipped her fingers free of his grasp and turned away.

Smiling what she hoped was an enigmatic smile, Ellen walked through the crowd and through the grand arched entrance of the palace ballroom. The crowd parted before her, making her escape dramatic and also quite fast.

Which was good, because as the clock ticked closer to midnight, something was happening to her shoes.

Down the palace steps, into the waiting carriage—a strange thing like a large round basket woven of gold, and pulled by an excess of horses. The mute coachman cracked his whip urgently, and the dozen white horses shot forward. Sensing his passenger's discomfort—or needing to get back to his mistress with just as much urgency—the coachman used his long whip to clear the road, while the horses with their crashing

hooves and shrill whinnies made the noise that their driver could not.

Sitting back on the white silk cushions, Ellen flexed her feet and groaned. The shoes were first hot, then cold, and tremors ran up her legs. The pliable glass was stiffening, and she reached down to take the shoes off but couldn't. Her feet cramped, and she whimpered.

An eternity later, but what was surely only minutes considering that Seadown House was just a few streets away, they reached the stable yard behind the manor. A bonfire had already been lit by a mute groom who was waiting nearby to toss a bucket of water on it.

The horses ran into the steam and soggy ash, and Ellen squeaked as the ground dropped away beneath them. The wheels of the carriage struck the glass floor of her godmother's palace with a crash, and she fell off the seat.

Her godmother rushed forward, clucking her tongue. "Cutting it fine, cutting it fine!" Her tone was both playful and scolding. "I hope this means that you were enjoying yourself, my lovely."

"Yes," Ellen said tremulously as a pair of footmen helped her out. "But the shoes!"

"Of course, my darling!"

Her godmother pulled out a small golden hammer and rapped it sharply on first one shoe, then the other. The pliable glass had grown quite hard as midnight came, and now the beautiful ruby-colored slippers shattered into a million tiny shards. Ellen's feet no longer tingled, instead they seemed numb

and cold, and her godmother had to help her step out of the circle of broken glass.

Then the silent servants rushed forward to divest the girl of gown and jewels. They jerked her housemaid uniform over her head and sent her back through the ashes into the garden without even fastening it.

Ellen didn't have time to say good-bye to her godmother, or thank her, before she staggered into the manor, dazed and half-dressed, to see that it was now two minutes past midnight. Her feet were still icy cold and she carried her underclothes, stockings, and shoes jumbled together in her arms. She had just enough time to put herself back together before the Seadowns arrived home, full of questions about Lady Ella.

Confused

Was her father an earl?"

"I don't know, Your Majesty," Christian said.

"A duke? A knight?"

"Honestly, King Rupert, I don't know. She wouldn't say. No family name, and not a hint of where I had met her before."

"Odd." King Rupert steepled his fingers.

"Very, Your Majesty," Christian said with a sigh. He and the king had been through this many times already, and it was only noon.

"But you seemed quite taken with her," King Rupert stated for the hundredth time.

"Yes, Your Majesty," Christian said, and then shook himself a little.

Why had he said that? Lady Ella was certainly pretty, but more than a little strange, in his opinion. And not the good kind of strange, like Poppy. Yet the first thing he had done that morning was to ask Queen Edith if she knew Lady Ella's family. That was what had started the endless round of questions by King Rupert. Christian could predict what was coming next.

"Bretoner? You're certain?" King Rupert leaned over his desk eagerly.

This was the most important question to the king, and he would never be satisfied until they had tracked down Lady Ella and had her write out her lineage to the twelfth generation, Christian was sure.

"Yes, Your Majesty," Christian said. "She had no accent and she said that she lived in Castleraugh. I believe that both Pop—Princess Poppy, that is—and Roger Thwaite know her."

"The princess wouldn't know: she isn't Bretoner," King Rupert said dismissively.

"True, however—," Christian began, but the king was off and running.

"We must make sure that this girl comes to our masked ball," King Rupert said, turning to gaze out the window at the royal gardens, face set with thought. "Everyone who was invited to the gala has also been invited to the masquerade, so that shouldn't be a problem. The difficulty will be recognizing her." He put his hands behind his back, eyes narrowed.

Christian wondered if he should just slip out. Or excuse himself and go. He wanted to visit Seadown House and talk to Poppy, though he could not remember why. Had he been planning on asking her about Lady Ella? No, that didn't seem right. He could always ask Roger Thwaite about that. Still, he would probably remember when he got there.

Just as Christian got to his feet, a footman knocked at the door and then entered carrying a silver tray.

"What's this?" King Rupert turned away from his window, irritated, and caught Christian in the act of escaping.

The footman, who valued his job too much to show any sign of surprise at the prince's guilty, frozen stance, merely presented the tray. "Today's correspondence, Your Majesty," the man said blandly.

One of the letters, a small creamy envelope with a blue seal on it, made the king turn to Christian. The prince, for his part, was wondering if he dared slip out of the room with the footman when the servant was dismissed.

"Seadowns are throwing a ball next week," King Rupert said. He grunted. "Trying to marry off that princess, do y'suppose?"

"It's Marianne's birthday," Christian said. He wondered if Lady Ella would be there. The Seadowns didn't seem to know her, but Poppy did.

"Oh yes," King Rupert said, and shrugged. "Should probably make an appearance. Send Edith and the girls at the least. You, too, I suppose. The Thwaites are already planning the marriage feast for the younger son and Lady Marianne, but no harm in trying if this Lady Ella proves unsuitable." The king was already turning back to the window, his mind elsewhere.

Christian beat a hasty retreat.

He also had an invitation to Marianne's ball waiting in his room, along with letters from his parents and sisters, and one, oddly, that came from Westfalin. The envelope was creased and water-stained, and the writing nearly illegible. He stuck it in

his pocket to read later, pulled on his riding boots, and went to pay a call on the Seadowns.

He had hardly ridden out of the palace gates before he was hailed by Roger and Dickon Thwaite, who both looked rather grim. Christian reined in to meet them, curiosity over their dire expressions winning out over disappointment at the distraction.

"What's happened? You look like you've had some bad news," Christian said.

"I say, Christian," Dickon said, shaking his head in puzzlement. "Did Lady Ella seem cursed to you? I thought she was charming, but Roger's gotten it into his head that she's under some sort of enchantment."

"An enchantment?" Alarm spread through Christian. "We must help her! Quickly, the palace has weapons we can use!"

"Capital! We'll need swords and pistols!" Dickon looked eagerly at his older brother, who was staring at both of them with consternation. "Coming, Roger?"

"You're both acting like idiots," Roger said, almost musingly. "This is perhaps part of it . . ."

"Part of what?" Christian steadied his horse with one hand. Why were they all sitting on horses in the middle of the street? Had they been on their way to the park? He turned his horse in that direction and the brothers flanked him, their horses moving at an easy walk. He felt his belt for a pistol, then couldn't remember why he would be armed.

"I believe that Lady Ella is under an enchantment," Roger

explained. "And I think it's spreading. The two of you are not behaving as you normally would, even around a beautiful young woman." He shot a sly glance at Christian, then at Dickon. "Especially considering that both your attentions should be elsewhere."

Dickon looked quite astonished. "Where do you mean?"

"Precisely," Roger said, much to Christian's confusion. But the older Thwaite brother did not appear to be teasing them or reveling in their bewilderment. Rather, he seemed to sink deeper into thought, a frown settling on his face and creasing his forehead. "Precisely."

"Look here, fellows," Dickon said eagerly. "Do you think if we ride around the park long enough, Lady Ella will put in an appearance? There's quite a few ladies out today."

Christian, too, was craning his neck for a glimpse of dark hair. He remembered Poppy then, and Marianne, and felt a jolt. He hadn't been riding to the park! He had been on his way to Seadown House. Feeling muzzy-headed and faintly embarrassed, he was about to suggest that they invite Marianne and Poppy to join them when Roger did it for him.

"I must speak with Princess Poppy," Roger announced. "Let's go out this way, toward the Seadowns'. Come to think of it, I should probably inform Lord Richard of my suspicions as well. And talk to El—talk to an old friend, if she is there."

Christian, relieved to have remembered his destination, didn't ask who in the Seadowns' household Roger considered

an old friend. Dickon, for his part, was so busy looking for Lady Ella that he was almost sitting backward in the saddle.

"She must be around here somewhere," the younger Thwaite kept muttering.

Finally Roger grabbed the reins of his brother's horse. "Just come along, Dickon, we'll get you sorted out later."

Investigator

Roger, thank heavens!" Poppy leaped to her feet, scattering her knitting across the floor, when the butler showed Christian, Roger, and Dickon into the parlor. "I just sent you a message!"

She barely stopped herself in time: she had been close to throwing her arms around the older Thwaite brother in relief. She looked at Christian, almost blushing, but he was glancing around the parlor as though he had never seen it before. Dickon Thwaite, too, looked around with an expression of mild interest, taking no notice of Marianne on the sofa. Poppy raised her eyebrows, and Roger nodded gravely.

"Dickon, Christian," Poppy said loudly. "Why don't you chat with Marianne while Roger and I discuss something?" She kept her voice bright yet firm. It was the same type of voice she used when trying to get Pansy and Petunia—her youngest sisters—to do something without any tantrums.

"Are you plotting something, Poppy?" Marianne looked up with a twinkle in her eye, her hands tangled in yarn.

Poppy had been trying to teach her to knit in order to distract Marianne from the two topics that obsessed her: her birthday ball and Lady Ella.

Marianne had awoken that morning with a pounding headache and a memory of the gala that differed from Poppy's. She remembered Lady Ella being not just pretty, but devastatingly beautiful, and both Christian and Dickon dancing only with the mysterious charmer, ignoring Poppy and herself entirely. She was almost violent in her feelings toward Lady Ella, and no amount of correction on Poppy's part would convince her that her memories were wrong.

Having given up trying to talk to her friend about enchantments and the truth behind Lady Ella's identity, Poppy had instead gotten her to talk about her own ball. She had hinted about gifts, both from herself and Marianne's parents, and even agreed to dance at least one dance, just to appease her friend.

Poppy explained all this in a rush to Roger as they took up a position by the window seat, half-hidden in the long purple drapes. Poppy found her eyes searching each passing carriage, as though she expected a familiar face to arrive and provide help. But the depressing truth was that no one was coming.

"But what about Eleanora?" Roger's voice was low.

"Oh yes! Eleanora!" Poppy was almost as passionate about her as Marianne was. "I insisted on coming home as soon as

she left the ballroom, hoping that we could catch her changing her gown or something. But having the carriage brought round took so blasted long that it was nearly one o'clock before we arrived. And there she was, waiting to help Marianne and me undress as though she hadn't been throwing herself at Christian just an hour before!"

"The gown? The jewels? There was no sign of them?"

"None at all," Poppy affirmed. "In fact, I stayed up until nearly dawn searching most of the house. And this morning I sneaked upstairs to look in the maids' rooms."

"Did you ask her about it directly? What did she say?"

" 'I don't know what you mean, Your Highness,' " Poppy recited. " 'I never left the manor, Your Highness. I wouldn't have a gown fit for a ball!' " Poppy gritted her teeth. "All sweet ignorance, and all of it a lie."

"Now, Your Highness," Roger said, flushing.

Poppy remembered belatedly that Ellen, no matter how trying, was Roger's childhood friend, and checked her temper. Slightly.

"Call me Poppy," she said. "And I'm afraid it's true. There was none of the nonsense that my sisters and I went through. She didn't start babbling incoherently, she didn't suddenly lose her voice. She looked right at me with big eyes and lied. Just as she lied when I asked her why, then, was her hair so full of pomade? Why did she smell of exotic perfume? And, more tellingly, where were her stockings and why was she limping?"

"Limping?"

Roger looked concerned, and Poppy had to fight down another sigh. It would not do for him to be just as smitten with "Lady Ella" as the other gentlemen, with or without enchantment.

"I would imagine it was from dancing for hours in those impractical shoes," she said. "I'm sure she'll be fine. In the meantime, we really must figure out what is happening."

"What is happening in here?"

Poppy and Roger looked up, startled, as Poppy's words were echoed from the doorway. Lord Richard had just come into the room, and was surveying the assorted young people with his typical amusement.

"Rehashing last night's gala? Gossiping about who danced with whom?"

Lord Richard had been in the garden with friends during most of the gala, and had not seen Lady Ella. But his ears had been filled with the story of how Poppy's gown had been copied by the mysterious upstart, as Marianne labeled her, all the way back to the manor the night before. More speculation had occurred over breakfast, of course, which caused the gentleman to barricade himself behind a newspaper.

"Papa," Marianne said peevishly. "There's no use ignoring it: Lady Ella ruined the effect of Poppy's gown and stole away all the gentlemen!" Marianne gave Dickon an uncharacteristically scornful look.

Clearly startled, Lord Richard studied his normally cheerful daughter and then glanced at Roger and Poppy before turning back to Marianne. "*All* the gentlemen? My dear, I hardly think

it possible for one young girl to commandeer *all* your dance partners at once."

Before Marianne could reply, Poppy took Roger by the arm and led him across the room. "Cousin Richard, if we might have a word with you in your study?"

Lord Richard nodded. "As you seem more yourself today than the rest of the household, I am quite agreeable," he said.

"What's this all about?" The earl hardly waited until the study door was shut to ask the question.

First Roger, then Poppy poured out everything they knew: how Eleanora the penniless orphan had become Ellen the maid, then gone to the ball in a gown copied from Poppy's and entranced everyone who saw her there. How no one, not even Lady Margaret, had recognized her, and how this morning Christian and Dickon were both muzzy-headed and obsessed with this Lady Ella, while Marianne and her mother both reviled the mystery woman for being so spectacular and desired.

"I can't find any sign of the gown, the slippers, none of it," Poppy said. "I've asked her over and over again about last night, but she denies everything."

Seated behind his grand desk, Lord Richard toyed with a letter opener. "I see." He pursed his lips. "Poppy, if I may ask a rather sensitive question: does this in any way recall the . . . unpleasantness you and your sisters suffered from?"

"Not at all," Poppy said promptly. "Oh, it feels like some kind of spell, but that's just my intuition. Ellen seems pleased. I believe that she could talk about it if she wanted to. I've seen

her walking around the manor at all hours of the night, and always covered in soot with an expression like the cat who stole the cream. You didn't see her last night, but I . . ."

She trailed off, finally noticing the expression on Lord Richard's face. He was quite gray, and his eyes were bleak.

"Did you say covered in soot?" His voice was hardly more than a whisper.

Poppy had to clear her throat twice before she answered. "Yes. Why?"

Lord Richard merely stared over their shoulders for a long time, then he looked down at his desk, still pale. "This is something to think about, indeed. How did you avoid falling under the enchantment?"

Poppy opened her mouth to counter his question with one of her own, but thought better and meekly said, "I have garters knit especially to protect me."

"And Thwaite? What about you?"

"I happened to be wearing a charm given to me by a magician, sir," Roger said quietly. He, too, had become silent in the face of Lord Richard's terrible expression.

"Good. Keep them with you at all times. Now if you'll both excuse me. I would like to speak to Ellen. Alone." He reached for the bell pull, and Poppy and Roger retreated to the parlor.

Now Poppy didn't know what to think. Lord Richard knew something, Ellen was quite possibly a willing participant in the spell and didn't want to talk about it, and Christian was alarmingly obsessed with "Lady Ella." The comfortable little

world she had known here in Breton just days before was all coming down around her ears.

"At least it wasn't my fault," she murmured. "Of course, it wasn't before, either, but that didn't help."

She wanted to write another letter to Galen and Rose—she had already sent one that morning—but it was futile. They wouldn't receive the letter for nearly two weeks, and it would be yet another two weeks before she had a reply.

She was both consoled and a little frightened, too, by Roger's look of shock. The consolation came from not being the only one thrown by Lord Richard's reaction. The fright, however, came from discovering that even with Roger's knowledge of spells and magic, and Lord Richard's steady intelligence, they hadn't found a ready answer for what was happening.

Back in the parlor, Christian was playing chess with Marianne while Dickon looked on. The scene was so much the way things had been before the royal gala that Poppy was quite reassured. If they could just avoid talking about Lady Ella until this was sorted out, everything might be all right after all.

Exchanging a relieved look with Roger, Poppy sat on the sofa and took up her knitting.

"I wonder if Lady Ella plays chess?" Dickon mused brightly.

Poppy cursed.

Torn

Ellen limped to his lordship's study, her heart thumping. Her feet were feeling better, but she had been upstairs when she was summoned and the long walk down the stairs had made them ache again. The soles felt scorched, and her toes were very stiff.

It reminded her of a holiday by the sea her family had taken when she was a child. She had pulled off her shoes and stockings and run down the shore, not realizing until she reached the edge of the water that the sand was blazingly hot beneath the midday sun.

But had been worth it to feel the waves curl up over her toes, and the pain today was worth it as well. She had danced with a prince, and he had hung on her every word. And she had danced with Roger Thwaite, who was just as handsome as she remembered from the days before her father's ruin. She had been the shining star of the royal gala, and Marianne and Poppy could not stop talking about it.

It was rather troubling that Poppy had recognized her, though, and suspected that magic was involved. Poppy seemed to think that Eleanora was in some kind of danger, and needed to be saved. She was quite odd, Ellen thought as she knocked softly on the door of Lord Seadown's study, momentarily distracted. Quite odd.

Her fears came rushing back as she heard Lord Seadown's voice bidding her to enter. He was sitting in a tall leather chair behind his desk, his expression severe. She shut the door and stood with her back against it, trying not to look guilty.

Then she raised her chin and took a step farther into the room, carefully placing her feet so their stiffness was not obvious. After all, she had nothing to feel guilty about. Lady Seadown had said she might go the royal gala, and the queen's birthday ball in two weeks. And she hadn't broken or burned anything (other than her feet) in two days.

"Yes, my lord?"

"Please sit down, Eleanora," Lord Richard said, and indicated one of the handsome green upholstered chairs across from his desk.

Startled that he knew her real name, Ellen sat. She clasped her hands in her lap, noticed a stain on her white apron, and moved her left arm a fraction to cover it. She resisted the urge to twiddle her thumbs, and tried to look his lordship in the eye.

She had done nothing wrong.

"My dear, it has come to my attention that you may be in some trouble," Lord Richard said gently.

"I don't know what you mean, sir," she said meekly.

"Perhaps you do not yet realize that you are in trouble," he said. He closed his eyes and looked pained. "My dear, making bargains with . . . persons of power, shall we say . . . is never wise. They always find ways to twist their promises.

"Princess Poppy can be rather brash, I know, and I believe that she may have confronted you today about last night's gala—"

"But your lordship! I didn't attend the gala," she protested, feeling a flush crawl up her neck and cheeks at the lie. "I haven't a gown for such things!"

She would not tell him about her godmother. He would think it was black magic, and try to stop her from going back. She had to see her godmother again. She had to have more gowns, and go to more balls, so she could marry Prince Christian and be taken far away from Seadown House and its endless piles of ironing.

Lord Richard looked at her as he would have looked at Marianne, had she disappointed him. "Does the name 'the Corley' mean anything to you?"

Ellen felt the flush run all the way up to her forehead, and then recede like a sudden tide, leaving her pale. How did he know her godmother's name? She swallowed, her throat dry.

"No," she whispered. "No, your lordship."

Lord Richard looked even more disappointed, and shockingly haggard. He stared into her eyes for a long time. Ellen wondered what horrifying tale someone had told him about her godmother that made him so frightened of the old woman. She

felt even more strongly that she must not tell him the truth. All her hopes would be dashed if she did.

"Are you certain?"

"Yes, your lordship." She smoothed her apron. "May I go, Lord Richard? I would not want to shirk my duties."

He hesitated, his eyes boring into hers. "Very well. But please, my dear, if you wish to discuss . . . anything, please come to me. Or to Poppy or Roger Thwaite. We only want to help you."

"Thank you, your lordship," she said calmly as she rose. "But I am quite well."

She managed to get out of the study without limping at all, and really did go downstairs to the airing room to collect the linens for ironing. That morning she had managed to make three beds without lumps or wrinkles, had carried a vase of flowers from the kitchen to the parlor without dropping the vase, crushing the flowers, or spilling any water, and had even taken a tea tray to Lady Margaret without incident.

Either dancing with Prince Christian had given her a new confidence, or her godmother was somehow watching out for her, Ellen thought as she ironed. The iron's temperature remained constant and the wrinkles smoothed down just as they should. There was no scorching of fabric, no burning of fingers. Ellen practically sang as she worked, and the stares of the other maids as she filled a basket with neatly ironed and folded linens couldn't dampen her spirits in the slightest. Even the soot that seemed to sift its way into the folds of her clothes and cover everything she touched was gone.

Her good mood was finally ruined, however, when she burst out of the passageway from the servants' domain and ran straight into Prince Christian. The basket of ironed linens between them, they gazed at each other, startled, for a moment.

Ellen's heart began to race, and the blood thrummed in her ears so loudly that it took her a moment to understand what he was saying to her. When she finally comprehended his words, she felt her cheeks burn even hotter.

"Pardon me," Prince Christian said again, and stepped around her. He whistled as he made his way to the water closet.

The complete lack of recognition in his face shook her. Had he not known her because of her maid's uniform? She turned it over and over in her mind as she went about the rest of her tasks that day.

Had he only looked at her clothes, and not at her face? Roger Thwaite had known her, known her the instant he had seen her at the ball. Poppy had known her as well, but Marianne and Lady Margaret hadn't recognized her and clearly thought that Poppy was mistaken.

Ellen's godmother had said that she would cast a "mild glamour" over her, so there would be no hue and cry over a maid attending the royal gala, but surely a mild glamour wouldn't prevent Prince Christian from knowing the dance partner he had been smitten with just hours before! Should she tell him? She would have to, eventually, if they were to be wed.

Worrying, too, was the cavalier way the Corley had shooed her out of her palace, aching feet and all. Ellen had hoped, deep down, that her godmother would let her stay in the glass-

pillared palace from now on. That she would be allowed to take on the role of Lady Ella all the time, and not return to being Ellen the maid.

But she would be attending Marianne's birthday ball as Lady Ella. And then there was the masked ball at the palace. By the end of the masquerade she would have a proposal of marriage and she could finally quit her maid's position for her new life.

With Prince Christian.

As she came down the stairs to the kitchen again, she caught a glimpse of a tall figure with dark hair coming out of the parlor. Her heart pounding, Ellen ducked behind a curtain and peeped out. It was Roger, and she didn't want him to see her in her maid's uniform. He would recognize her, she felt certain.

He would recognize her no matter what she wore.

Through her high-necked gown she fingered the little garnet ring on its chain. Roger had given it to her for her twelfth birthday and she had worn it every day since. It was too small for any of her fingers now, so she wore it around her neck on a ribbon along with the locket containing her mother's portrait. She had had to hide both of these from her father during the final days of his ruin. Neither piece of jewelry was worth very much money, but they had needed every pound and the earl would have pawned them without a thought for the grief it would have caused his daughter.

From her hiding place, Ellen could see that Roger was with Poppy, and she felt a stab of jealousy. They moved close

to the stairs just below where Ellen stood, and she strained to listen.

"He's already spoken to her, and she's gone," Poppy said.

"From the house?" Roger sounded alarmed.

"No, just from his study," Poppy said. "But he won't tell me what she said."

"He's deeply disturbed by all this."

"I've been wondering," Poppy said, but then stopped.

"Yes?" Roger moved closer to her, and Ellen gritted her teeth.

"I've been wondering about Lord Richard's gambling."

"But he doesn't gamble," Roger pointed out.

"He doesn't *anymore,*" Poppy said. "But he used to, and he always won. And then one day he just quit. Do you think, perhaps, that he made some deal with a magician or someone like that, so that he would always win?"

"It's possible, I suppose," Roger mused. "And it was when you said that Eleanora was always covered in soot that he turned pale. Perhaps he has an idea who Eleanora might have dealt with."

"If that's so, then it can't have been someone very nice," Poppy said. "I've never seen Lord Richard look so frightened."

"But why isn't Eleanora frightened, then?"

"Possibly because she's too foolish to know better," Poppy said. Ellen's jaws were clenched so tightly together now that her teeth squeaked. "But possibly because she hasn't seen the true face of what she's dealing with yet. Black magic can appear harmless when it wants to."

"Very true," Roger said. Then he and Poppy moved toward the front door and she showed him out.

Ellen came out of her hiding place, straightened her cap where the curtain had knocked it askew, and marched down the steps as though she hadn't just been cowering at the top of them, eavesdropping. As Poppy came back across the entrance hall, she caught Ellen's eye but didn't say anything. Ellen bobbed a curtsy at the princess, then went through the little door under the stairs that led to the servants' quarters.

Perhaps her godmother was a little unfeeling about Ellen's hurt feet, or her desire to be rid of her maid's uniform for good. But why would she help Ellen at all if she didn't want her goddaughter to make a brilliant marriage and live happily with a prince till the end of her days?

It wasn't as if the Corley stood to benefit!

Magician

Why does magic always smell so awful?" Poppy lifted the lid of the pot and then dropped it back with a clatter. "This is making my eyes water!"

"Then stop lifting the lid!" Roger, in shirtsleeves, frowned at her. Or perhaps he was just frowning at the book propped open before him. He picked up a bundle of herbs, pulled off three leaves, and lifted the lid himself to throw them in.

Holding her nose when the steam wafted toward her, Poppy watched him with watering eyes. They were in the still-room at the Thwaites' manor, using an ancient text Roger had picked up on his travels to concoct a potion that would release the drinker from the Corley's spell.

Or so they hoped.

Roger's grasp of Shijn, the language of the text, was fairly good, but he was by no means fluent. And there was no guarantee that this would work on the Corley's specific enchantment. It was meant to be a cure for love sickness, which was the nearest thing they could find to the Ella obsession that their friends suffered from. Even now, Dickon was upstairs, writing sonnets to his new love, while back at Seadown House, Marianne was writing "Ella" on scraps of paper and then burning them.

Catching herself reaching for the lid again, Poppy retreated to the far side of the room and took up her knitting. She was doing her own little spell, knitting unbleached wool into bands that could be worn as bracelets. She wore garters of a similar make, and, itchy as they were, she had slept in them the last few nights to quell her nightmares. It had helped, and she hoped she could protect her friends in the same way.

"Another one done," she announced, casting off the end of the bracelet and cutting the dangling tail of yarn.

She dropped the strip of knitted wool into a pot of rainwater that contained three others. Measuring the remaining yarn, she saw she had enough left for one more bracelet, but only if she knitted so tightly her needles would squeak.

Roger stopped frowning over the Shijn text and frowned at her pot of bracelets and rainwater instead. It looked like eel stew, Poppy thought, and she didn't blame him for frowning. However, if he said anything disparaging . . .

"Now I add basil and nightshade and mint," she told him. "Which is another ghastly combination of odors certain to put me off dinner."

"Where did you learn about this?" He gave her a sidelong look. "I assume it was part of your family's defense against the King Under Stone, but how did you come by the knowledge?"

"Walter Vogel, one of our gardeners, was a white magician," Poppy said. "He told Galen, who is married to Rose now, about basil being good for protection, and nightshade for warding off enchantments. Galen read about adding mint later. It gives you clarity of mind."

"Interesting." Roger prodded the mint leaves on the table next to the pot. "So this Galen has continued studying magic?"

She moved the mint away with the tip of one needle. "Yes," she said. "Walter disappeared after Galen and Rose got married, but we found a trunk full of spell books in one of the garden sheds." She set aside her knitting. Trying to make the stitches tight enough that she wouldn't run out of yarn was tiring, and she wanted to get the other bands done as soon as she could.

Commandeering another of the small spirit burners, she put her pot of rainwater and knitting over it and began adding liberal bunches of mint, basil, and nightshade. It hadn't been easy finding nightshade in Castleraugh. For one thing, it had taken Poppy an hour and several dictionaries to figure out the Bretoner word for it, since her governess had never taught her to translate the names of deadly poisons. Then she'd had to find an apothecary that would sell it to her.

Many carried it, but only one would hand it over to the princess, who had been on the verge of hiring a thief to get her some by the time she found a shop seedy enough. The one-eyed shopkeeper had laughed during the entire transaction, as though delighted at the idea of her poisoning someone. When

she'd assured him that she only wanted it for medicinal purposes, he'd blinked at her in a way that she guessed passed for a wink, and laughed even harder.

"How much of that are you supposed to put in?" Roger watched her throwing in the herbs with narrowed eyes.

"I really don't think there's a measurement," Poppy said breezily. "We usually just toss some in. It's also good to keep fresh nightshade and basil with you, in your pockets maybe. Although you smell like an herb garden if you do."

"Interesting," Roger said again.

But Poppy could tell that he didn't think it interesting so much as dubious. He was so precise about everything that she knew watching her throw her herbs in willy-nilly was making him twitch. She added the last of the basil and put a lid on the pot.

"How is yours coming?" She nodded at his concoction.

Roger ponderously checked his pocket watch, then took the lid off the pot and stirred it with a long silver spoon. He sniffed the horrid stuff, checked with the text one last time, then took the pot off the burner.

"It should be ready," he said.

"How do we test it?"

Poppy's voice was high and nasal, since she had pinched her nose when he took the lid off the pot. The reek of it was really terrible, like unwashed feet, mushrooms, and cinnamon mixed together. Combined with the basil and mint from her pot, she had to fight to keep from gagging, and thanked the heavens that the nightshade, at least, was odorless.

"I'll give some to Dickon," Roger said. He wasn't holding his nose, but his face was rather greenish.

"If the ingredients are wrong, it won't kill him, will it?"

"It shouldn't; none of the ingredients are harmful."

"Other than the smell," she quipped.

"This should simmer overnight," she went on, indicating her pot. "I need some fresh air."

"Agreed," Roger said.

They both stumbled out of the stillroom and took great gulps of laundry-scented air in the adjacent drying room. When the potion had cooled, Roger went back into the still-room and poured it into a glass for Dickon.

"Will he drink it?"

"I'll tell him it's Lady Ella's favorite tea," Roger said.

Poppy laughed, and was still laughing when they went into the library. Dickon was awash in crumpled paper, and looked up with a dazed expression as they came in.

"Can you think of a rhyme for 'Ella' other than 'fella'?" he asked.

Poppy put one hand over her eyes. She could think of a number of things, like "yella," that would rhyme, but none of them made for good poetry. She didn't even want to know what was on the crumpled papers littering the table and floor.

"Poetry isn't really my strong suit," Roger said blandly. "Have a drink to refresh yourself, why don't you?"

"Ah, yes! Just the thing!"

Dickon reached for the tumbler eagerly enough, but when

the odor reached his nostrils he recoiled, nearly spilling it. Roger grabbed the glass back just in time.

"I say! It smells like an old boot!"

Roger started to say something about Lady Ella, but Poppy stopped him with a hand on his sleeve.

"Dickon," she said with a smile, "it's a love potion."

"Pardon?" the brothers said together.

"It will make you irresistible to Lady Ella."

"Really?" Dickon licked his lips, then shuddered. "Do you think I need it? I would much rather woo her with my poems."

Poppy felt her nostrils flare and she bit back a giggle. "Well, in case you can't find a rhyme for 'Ella' . . ." She took the glass from Roger and held it out to Dickon.

"Are you certain it will work?" He stopped with one hand outstretched. "Why does it smell so ghastly?"

"Because it only works on Lady Ella," Poppy improvised. "We strained it through one of her stockings."

"How did you get one of Lady Ella's stockings?"

"We bribed her maid. Now drink!"

Dickon hesitated only a second more, then he snatched the glass, gulped it down, and gagged. He fumbled the glass to the tabletop, holding his throat with his free hand.

"Oh! You've poisoned me!"

"Nonsense," Roger said in a worried voice. "You just have to, um, twist the glass." He made a wringing motion.

"Twist the glass?" Now it was Poppy and Dickon who spoke

at the same time. Dickon, still retching, obediently turned the glass around on the table.

"That's doing nothing," Poppy reported, twisting her own hands in the skirt of her gown.

"*Din yun, din yun . . . ?*" Roger pulled at his lower lip. "Oh!" He shook his head. "*Throw* the glass!"

"With pleasure," Dickon choked, and tossed the tumbler into the hearth.

The glass shattered into tiny diamonds, which smoked and disappeared with a gentle chiming sound. Poppy closed her mouth, and looked to Dickon, who all at once sat up in his chair and looked around as if he'd just awakened.

"What was that for?"

"So you'd stop making a fool of yourself with Lady Ella," Poppy said, carefully watching for his reaction.

"Lady Ella? That strange girl who kept hitting Christian with her fan?" Dickon shook his head and turned back to his papers and pen. "Don't know what you mean. Now kindly leave me in peace while I compose a letter to Marianne. Her birthday is tomorrow, you know."

Roger and Poppy fled to the hallway where they stood, looking stunned, for a moment.

"Goodness," Poppy said at last. "That seemed too easy."

Dreamer

Poppy stood up in the middle of her bed, just to make sure she didn't fall back asleep and continue her wretched, wretched nightmare. Why she had to endlessly visit the Palace Under Stone she didn't know, but she hoped the dreams would stop soon.

She crouched down and reached under her pillow to make sure the little white sachet was still there. It was. She plucked it out and held it to her nose. Still fragrant with herbs after all these years, the muslin bag had been a gift from Walter Vogel. He had given sachets to Poppy and all her sisters some ten years ago, to ward off bad dreams. Hers didn't seem to be working anymore, though it still smelled as fresh as always.

Something else to write to Galen about. Poppy wished she could ask Walter, but his work in Westfalin was done, though Poppy and her sisters still missed the strange old man. She wondered if there was some way to summon him, for surely his knowledge of magic was needed here in Breton now.

She got up and wrote a note to Galen and Rose, including the strange dream, the questions about her sachet, and the possibility of reaching Walter Vogel. She sealed and addressed it so that it could go out with the first post, but even so it would reach Galen and Rose far too late to help. Marianne's birthday ball was only two days away, and Poppy was sure that "Lady Ella" would be in attendance, causing even more mayhem than before.

Christian and Lady Margaret could talk of little else, and Marianne burst into tears whenever anyone mentioned either Ella or the royal gala. Dickon had needed two more doses of the potion, which seemed to wear off after a day, and Roger was frantically trying to brew more of the malodorous stuff, but was having trouble locating one of the ingredients. And the Thwaite's stillroom maid had turned off the spirit lamp under Poppy's pot of boiling wool, and now she would have to start all over again with the herbs and rainwater.

Roger had come to the house twice specifically to call on Ellen and try to winkle out her plans for the upcoming ball, but both times the girl conveniently vanished.

But when Poppy saw the dress that Lady Margaret had had made for her to wear to Marianne's ball, she resolved that she would confront Ellen in front of all the guests if "Lady Ella" wore a copy of it.

It was of deep violet satin with an overskirt of smoky gray tissue that softened the color underneath and made Poppy look and feel like a fairy princess. There was silver embroidery around

the neckline, and matching satin shoes. She already had a violet silk choker she wore to enliven a white gown she had inherited from Lily.

"And look at mine," Marianne burbled, her thoughts taken away from Lady Ella for the first time all day. "Just look!"

Poppy looked, and applauded. Marianne would outshine everyone in such a gown, and Poppy felt some of the tension in her shoulders unknot. Marianne's gown was rose-colored satin with a faint tracery of gold embroidery around the sleeves and hem. Lady Margaret was going to let Marianne wear the pearl tiara and necklace—each with a single pink diamond as a centerpiece—that had been her wedding gift from Lord Richard.

Poppy twirled Marianne around. "You'll be gorgeous!"

"Yes, gorgeous, Lady Marianne," echoed a voice from the doorway. Ellen stood there with a tea tray in her hands and a funny little smile on her face.

Poppy took the tray before Ellen contrived to spill the tea on either gown. Although Ellen had been remarkably graceful of late, Poppy was taking no chances.

"Don't even think about it," Poppy warned as Ellen's blue eyes lit on the silver and violet gown.

"*I* won't," Ellen retorted, curtsied, and sidled out.

"There's no need to be harsh," Lady Margaret said gently.

Knowing that Lady Margaret still wouldn't believe her, and not wanting to weather the floods of tears from Marianne that a mention of Lady Ella would bring, Poppy apologized.

Then she turned her attention back to the ball gowns, admiring the fine stitching and dramatic layers of skirts.

But Lady Margaret was still staring at the closed door with an expression of concern on her face. "I just don't know what to do about that girl," she murmured. "She wanted to attend the royal gala so badly; but now she appears perfectly satisfied in not having gone."

"Her maid skills seem to be improving," Marianne said, fingering the pink rosettes on the bodice of her new gown. "Maybe she's finally become resigned to being in service."

"I really don't think that's it," Poppy said, but declined to discuss it any further.

Christian would return to the Danelaw the week after the royal masked ball, and Lady Ella clearly had set her cap for the prince, which meant that something was likely to happen at that masked ball or soon after. But they had no idea what, and if Ellen wouldn't talk to them, there was nothing they could do to prevent it.

Nothing but wait, and watch, and hope the foolish girl came to her senses and confided the secret of her enchantment to them, and soon.

~

"Who does she think she is?" Marianne was livid with rage. The flush made her look even prettier, but Poppy doubted that her friend would appreciate a compliment right now.

Lady Ella had indeed come to Marianne's birthday ball, arriving late and in grand style in a large golden carriage

pulled by a dozen gleaming white horses and attended by half a dozen handsome but mute servants. She had swept into the ballroom and gone immediately to Christian, who had dropped Marianne's hand like a hot brick and instead squired Lady Ella during the opening dance.

The entire room, the entire manor, was silent with shock through most of that first dance. Then the babbling had broken out: the questions, the speculation, the compliments and insults. The gentlemen were even more enamored of Ellen than before, Poppy noticed, while the ladies were more vicious. But Poppy couldn't blame them: not only was she stealing the limelight from Marianne, but she was dressed, purposely, to outshine her.

Rather than copying Poppy's gown, this time Ella had copied Marianne's.

"I don't care how fond you are of her," Poppy said to Roger as they stood to one side of the dance floor. Marianne whirled past them, partnered by her father now, her face red and eyes shining with unshed tears. "I might have to kill her."

Lady Ella and Christian were leading the figures of the dance, a whirl of black suit and rose-satin gown. As Ella's skirts swirled, tantalizing glimpses of her gleaming shoes were revealed. They were rose and gold, and once more looked like nothing so much as exquisitely blown glass. Her necklace and tiara were more opulent versions of Lady Seadown's, worn by Marianne with such pride.

"This is not like her," Roger said uneasily.

"No, this is not like your memory of her," Poppy corrected him.

"I still can't believe she would do something so deliberately cruel," Roger said, shaking his head.

"People change," Poppy said under her breath. "Let's go have a look at her carriage. As soon as this dance ends, I want you to ask her to dance. Insist, if you must. And try to get some answers."

Swallowing, Roger nodded and followed Poppy out into the night air to look at the carriage of gold with its silent coachmen and its even more eerily silent horses. As the cold air cooled Poppy's hot cheeks, she tried to tell herself she was only upset on Marianne's behalf, and not because Christian was making such a fool of himself.

Dizzy

Christian danced across the Seadowns' ballroom with Lady Ella in his arms. Everyone was watching them, and he knew precisely why: Lady Ella was the most stunning young woman in all of Castleraugh—no, in all of Breton!

It was a pity that Marianne Seadown had tried to copy Lady Ella's gown, but really, she couldn't hope to compete. She looked quite sweet in her pink gown, but Lady Ella's was so clearly of a richer fabric, the gold threads flashing boldly, that poor Marianne just looked washed out.

The only thing that dampened his enjoyment was that Lady Ella was being just as coy this evening as she had been at the royal gala. She would not tell him her family name or where she lived, and she wouldn't make any plans to meet with him outside of the ball.

"Won't you at least meet me in the park for a ride? Or if you do not ride, we could walk," he wheedled.

"Oh, no, Your Highness," she said with a flirtatious smile.

"I'm afraid that my guardian is so very strict, she will not let me go anywhere!"

"She let you come here tonight," Christian said with a burst of inspiration. "And without a chaperone!" He looked at her in triumph.

"Well, the Seadowns are old friends," she replied evasively. "So of course I'm permitted to come to La—Marianne's ball."

Something about this nagged at Christian's brain. If she and Marianne were friends, why did Marianne look so upset? And why had none of the Seadowns greeted Ella when she arrived? It all seemed quite irregular.

"I do wish people weren't giving me such awful looks," Lady Ella fretted.

"They're just jealous because you are so beautiful," Christian assured her.

Something silver and lavender flashed in the corner of his eye. Blinking rapidly, he had the unpleasant reminder of all those green flashes he had been seeing since he arrived in Breton. They had, thank the heavens, stopped a week or two ago, but the silver and lavender flash brought back the strange feeling of being watched.

He turned to see where it had come from, and saw Poppy standing at the doorway of the ballroom. She gave him a brief look of something—pity? Annoyance? It was hard to say. Then she went out with Roger Thwaite on her heels.

Where were they going? Christian stumbled a little, trying to crane his neck to watch. Surely if they were sneaking off for a tryst they wouldn't have left the ballroom together? He

stumbled again, and stepped on one of Lady Ella's feet. Letting out a faint scream, she collapsed against him.

Christian leaped back in embarrassment, holding the sagging Lady Ella by her elbows. "I'm so sorry! Are you all right?"

Several of the other dancers bumped into them, causing confusion and laughter from those watching. Mortified, Christian half-carried Lady Ella from the dance floor to a chair where she could rest.

"Did I break your foot?" Christian hadn't stepped on the toes of a dance partner since his first ball at the age of twelve, and now he had probably crippled poor Lady Ella! What had he been thinking, letting his attention wander off after Poppy? As though Poppy's relationship with Roger Thwaite was anything to do with him!

Dragging his attention back to Lady Ella, he knelt by her feet. "May I look?"

She was slumped back in the chair. "You must think I'm such a goose," she said faintly.

"Not at all." Feeling very daring, Christian delicately folded back the hem of her pink gown.

"What happened to your feet?" he asked in a hushed voice.

It made him blush even more, but he couldn't help himself. Lady Ella wasn't wearing stockings, which was rather embarrassing in and of itself. All along the edge of the shoes her feet were white, and not just the white of pale skin. But white like marble, and equally slick-looking.

"What is wrong with them?"

Lady Ella seemed to come to herself. She gasped and

straightened in her chair, shaking down her skirts. Her pale cheeks turned as pink as her gown.

"Oh, Your Highness! Really, I am quite all right! There is no need for you to worry," she babbled.

"If there is no need for you to worry, Prince Christian, then perhaps you had better go find your next partner," Lady Margaret said sternly as she glided up to them. She gave Lady Ella a hard look.

"I think I should stay with Lady Ella," Christian said staunchly as he stood. He smoothed his jacket and smiled at Lady Margaret, but she didn't return the smile.

"Really, Your Highness," Lady Margaret said, voice tight. "You don't want the other young ladies to feel neglected! And all the young men want a dance with Lady Ella. Mustn't be selfish." This last comment should have sounded teasing, but coming through gritted teeth it sounded rather menacing instead.

"But His Highness has insisted on filling my dance card," Lady Ella said, her eyes lowered demurely.

"But if you cannot dance," Lady Margaret said with that same edge to her voice, "it is hardly fair."

By now Christian was so uncomfortable he was fighting an urge to flee the ballroom. But he bowed gallantly to Lady Ella and then his hostess. "Why do you not take a rest, Lady Ella, and I will dance with Lady Marianne?"

"Lovely," Lady Margaret said, grabbing Christian's arm before he could change his mind.

"I shall return shortly," he called over his shoulder to Lady Ella, who was looking bereft. He watched, almost stepping on Lady Margaret's feet now, as a swarm of young men surrounded Lady Ella. To his satisfaction, however, she continued to peer through the crowd of suitors after him.

"Marianne," Lady Margaret said as the first notes of the next dance began. "Here is His Highness." She practically shoved Christian into her daughter's lap.

Christian took Marianne's hand in his and led her onto the floor, feeling fuzzy and irritable. Lady Margaret was known for her grace and kindness, so why was she being so stern this evening? Nothing seemed to make sense, and he stumbled his way through a reel with Marianne—still red-eyed and looking daggers over at Lady Ella—having to guide him through the relatively simple steps.

As he saw Dickon Thwaite lean solicitously over Lady Ella, both he and Marianne nearly stumbled together. Then Lady Ella lifted the hem of her skirts just a little, to let Dickon see her feet. A flash of shining pink shoe, and Christian felt the floor rising up to meet him.

The next thing he knew, Poppy and Marianne were bending over him, and Roger Thwaite was shouting for everyone to step back and give Christian room to breathe. Everything seemed to swirl, and Christian shut his eyes again. When he opened them, there were three dark-haired girls leaning over him, and he thought he might be sick.

The girl with the blackest hair and a gown of purple and

silver, though he could not remember her name, was trying to pull up his sleeve. He opened his mouth to ask her what she was doing, and she frowned at him.

"Wear this," she said curtly. "And stop making a fool of yourself!" She tied something itchy on his wrist, then patted the back of his hand. "I hope this works," she muttered.

"What? Where is Lady Ella?"

Poppy lurched to her feet and, taking Marianne's arm, drew the other girl away. Their dark heads were inclined toward one another, and both girls were very pale.

Christian didn't even have time to look at the thing on his wrist before Roger Thwaite was holding a tumbler of something odorous to his lips. Christian gagged, and Roger poured the stuff down his throat and then pushed the empty glass into Christian's hand. Christian thrust the glass away, and it shattered on the polished floor of the ballroom, the broken pieces disappearing almost at once.

Christian wiped his mouth on the back of his hand as his vision cleared, and accepted Roger's hand up. He was so embarrassed by the evening's events that he wanted to crawl under a sofa and hide. Lady Ella fluttered around him, and he was pleased to see that she appeared none the worse now for his having trod on her toes.

"Are you quite well, Your Highness?" She brushed at his lapels and straightened his hair for him.

"Yes, I feel fine." Her touch on his head was soothing, and he felt a surge of energy course through him. He disengaged himself from Roger's hand. "Thank you, I'm all right," he

said stoutly to the older Thwaite brother, who was looking at him with deep concern.

"Are you certain?"

"Oh, I feel fine!" Christian straightened his jacket. "In fact, I should apologize to Marianne, and let her pick another dance. I don't want to ruin her birthday ball!"

Roger blinked at Christian in surprise, and Christian wondered what was wrong with him. This was Marianne's night, and he owed her an apology. Roger, with his impeccable manners, should appreciate that.

"And I'm still trying to get Poppy to give in and dance with me," Christian continued.

Now both Lady Ella and Roger were staring at him.

"But remember, Your Highness," Lady Ella broke in. "You promised to dance all the dances with me. And my foot has quite recovered!" She tapped him fiercely with her fan to call his attention to her fully.

"Are you hurt?" Roger's sharp eyes were on Lady Ella in a heartbeat. "Should you be dancing?"

"I—I'm fine," she stammered. She opened her fan and began waving it vigorously in front of her face, avoiding Roger's gaze. If Christian hadn't known better he would think that she had feelings for Roger.

"Well," Christian said, "as I've said: I would hate to be rude to Marianne on her special night. Perhaps you wouldn't mind so much taking to the floor with Roger on this next dance, while I make things up to Marianne at the least?"

More vigorous fanning, and then a sigh.

"I'm sorry, Your Highness," Lady Ella said, almost reluctantly. "But you and I were to dance all the dances tonight. Together."

Her voice faded out on the last word, and Christian felt even more confused than he had been over Roger's and Poppy's behavior. He couldn't believe that he had been so dizzy he'd forgotten Poppy's name. He was profoundly relieved that he hadn't said something to give his momentary lapse away. She would have teased him for months!

The reel had ended and another dance began: a Bretoner jig. Neither of them very enthusiastic, Christian and Lady Ella joined the other couples on the floor. His dizziness and that strange feeling of having his brain packed in wool had faded, but Lady Ella still winced when the steps of the dance were too strenuous. He wished he had a moment to take off the bracelet Poppy had given him. It itched like mad, and only good manners kept him from dropping one of Lady Ella's hands so he could scratch it properly.

Spy

Marianne still didn't want to ruin the effect of her gown by putting on the bracelet that Poppy offered her, but after Christian fainted, Poppy managed to drag her friend into the ladies' salon. There, to the various looks of shock and amusement from the other ladies, Poppy at last convinced Marianne to hike up her skirts and wind it around her left garter.

"Must it always be about yarn with you?" Marianne complained. "Besides, it's itchy."

"It's wool," Poppy said. "And drink this for good measure, please." She reached behind a potted plant and retrieved a glass tumbler full of something that smelled like a combination of peaches and bacon and old stockings.

"Ugh! Why do I have to drink that . . . what is that?"

"Something Roger concocted, just to make doubly sure you are untouched by the enchantment," Poppy said, holding the glass as far from herself as she could. "Plug your nose and it won't be too bad. I drank some earlier."

"What enchantment?" Marianne was turning faintly green as the smell reached her.

"Exactly," Poppy said, swirling the contents of the cup a little. The liquid was sluggish and made a glopping noise. "It will be over in one gulp, and then you'll see what's really happening."

"All right," Marianne said doubtfully. She plugged her nose with one hand, took the glass with the other, and drank. "Oh, it's awful!" She thrust the glass at Poppy.

"Break the glass," Poppy said, refusing to take it.

"What?"

"Throw the glass down and break it, to finish the spell."

"All right," Marianne said, sounding as though she were just humoring Poppy. She dropped the glass on the carpeted floor without much enthusiasm. It bounced, rolled against an iron table leg, and cracked.

Marianne gave an unladylike grunt and looked at Poppy as though she'd been struck between the eyes. "Ellen is Lady Ella! She copied my dress! I'll brain her!"

Poppy let out her breath in a whoosh of relief.

"Why didn't you tell me before?" Marianne turned on Poppy in indignation.

"I did try," Poppy protested. "You didn't understand. It's part of the spell, so remember: do not take off that thing I knitted you! That's what's keeping you from succumbing to the enchantment again. The stinky drink might wear off in a day or so; we're hoping the bracelets will extend its protection. Tell me or Roger if you start to feel strange."

"All right," Marianne said. "Have you got something for my mother and father?"

"Your father doesn't need anything," Poppy said. "The enchantment doesn't work on him."

"Why is that?" Marianne goggled at Poppy as they went back to the ballroom.

"I don't know," Poppy said, squinting at the dancers. "But Roger and I are doing all we can to—There she goes, quick!"

The dance had ended. Lady Ella had looked at the clock at the end of the ballroom and was now excusing herself to Christian. Poppy checked the clock, too, and saw that it was a quarter to midnight; roughly the same time that Lady Ella had left the gala the week before.

The princess saw Roger standing near the entrance hall and signaled to him with her fan. The ballroom was crowded and people were taking notice of Marianne's return to the party. Poppy wasn't sure she would be able to make it to the door in time to see where Ella went.

But Roger faded out through the doors just before Ella got there, with Christian as well as several other satellite admirers still trailing her. Poppy turned Marianne over to the sympathetic ladies who surrounded them, and aimed herself at the door out of the ballroom with as much speed as she could muster, considering the people in her way and the heavy gown she was wearing.

Poppy got outside just as the strange, basketlike gold carriage was leaving with Lady Ella. Roger was sitting in his own small buggy, which he had had brought around just behind

Lady Ella's carriage and held at the ready. Poppy scrambled up onto the seat beside him, cursing and hoping fervently that she didn't ruin her new gown, and Roger whipped the horses forward.

He was wearing a large cloak over his evening clothes, and an old-fashioned three-cornered hat he had borrowed from a coachman. He took the reins in one hand and pulled a dark carriage rug from under the seat with the other. Poppy spread it over her light-colored gown.

Earlier, before Christian had fainted, Poppy and Roger had gone outside to see if they could get any information out of Lady Ella's servants. The carriage was easy enough to spot: no one had ever seen the like before and the horses gleamed so bright and white that they didn't look real.

But not only were all of Lady Ella's servants mute, their expressions were so hostile that Poppy found herself backing away, and the coachman went so far as to brandish his whip at Roger when the young man continued to snoop around the carriage. So Roger had a groom get his buggy ready and slip it into the queue of waiting carriages so they could follow Ella when she left.

And now they were racketing through Castleraugh after the golden carriage, which was traveling at an insane speed. It was fortunate that there were a number of carriages about this night, or it would have been very noticeable that they were being followed.

After a number of twists and turns, the golden carriage and the buggy following it had to slow down as they entered a

well-lit but narrow alley that ran behind some very fine manors. Looking around in confusion, Poppy recognized the back of one of the enormous houses.

"We're behind Seadown House," she hissed to Roger, who nodded.

After their wild chase through the streets, they had looped right back to where they had started out, or almost. Normally those riding in the carriages were let out in the front of the house, not back in the mews.

To Poppy's continued consternation, Lady Ella's golden carriage drove through the Seadowns' back gate. Where could Ellen possibly hide a team of horses, a golden coach, and half a dozen servants?

Roger stopped the buggy in the alley close to the fence, and they stood up to look over at what was happening in the back courtyard. A large bonfire had been built near the kitchen garden, but had fallen to ash. As they watched, the coachman drove the horses straight for this ashy, cindery mess.

Poppy almost cried out: the red heart of the bonfire was still visible, and the horses would be burned for certain. But Roger put a hand on her arm to stop her, and they watched in awe as the horses unfalteringly walked through the remains of the fire and disappeared, followed by the golden coach with coachman, footmen, Ella, and all.

"Did you see that?" Poppy's voice was barely a whisper.

"Yes," Roger replied, sounding just as shaken.

Poppy had never seen anything like it before. The entrance to the Kingdom Under Stone had been magical, true, but she

had known it her whole life. This was something else entirely, making a coach and horses and servants all disappear before you could blink, and Poppy's confidence crumbled in the face of it. What did she know, really, about breaking such a spell?

Nothing.

"We need to tell Lord Richard," she whispered.

"I agree."

Roger pulled his buggy through the gate and gave the reins to a startled groom who came sleepily out of the stable with straw in his hair when Roger shouted. Poppy asked him about the bonfire, and he looked at it as if he had never seen such a thing in his life.

They went into the manor through the kitchen and sent a maid to fetch Lord Richard. Poppy didn't want to get trapped among the guests once more, so they slipped along the passageway and into His Lordship's study.

Lord Richard came in a moment later, looking elegant in his evening clothes but with a line between his brows that hadn't left since Poppy and Roger had told him about Lady Ella the week before.

"She left at a quarter to midnight," Poppy said without preamble. There was, of course, no need to explain who she meant. "She got into a carriage made of gold, pulled by twelve white horses and manned by mute servants in white livery. We followed in Roger's buggy, and I don't think they noticed us. The coachman drove through the streets at breakneck speed for ten minutes or so, then doubled back and drove into the mews behind the manor. There was a bonfire

there in the courtyard, or the remains of one. The carriage drove into the ashes and vanished." She sat down in one of the high-backed leather chairs and folded her hands in her lap, watching Lord Richard's face.

The handsome older man merely nodded. He looked at the ornate clock over the fireplace and nodded again. He reached out and pulled the bell, and they all sat in silence until a maid came.

"Lydia, please send Ellen to me," Lord Richard said.

"Oh no! What's she broken now?" Lydia grimaced.

"Nothing," Lord Richard said mildly. "I merely need to speak with her."

"Yes, Your Lordship." She bobbed a curtsy and went out.

"You're still not surprised by any of this," Poppy said.

"I'm afraid not," her host said. "I see that you have given charms and the potion to both Christian and Marianne," he said, changing the subject.

"Yes." Poppy followed the transition, seeing that he was not going to explain himself further. At least until Ellen arrived. Behind her, she heard Roger stir, and he finally sat in the other seat across from the desk. "And just in time, too. They were both behaving quite foolishly."

"I don't think that fainting is foolish on Christian's part," Roger said. "I think it's a sign that things are terribly wrong."

"Is that what happened?" Lord Richard frowned. "I wasn't able to see."

"The combination of the potion and Poppy's knitted charm appears to have done the trick," Roger said.

"But he was still a bit taken with Ella . . . Ellen . . . whatever she wants to be called." Poppy wrinkled her nose and tried to keep her voice steady. "What if we can't break the spell permanently? We've had to give Dickon three doses of the potion so far, and he hasn't gotten as close to her as Christian."

"Well," Roger huffed. "It's not entirely out of the question that Christian has feelings for Eleanora *despite* the enchantment, you know. She is very beautiful, and—"

He was interrupted by a soft scratching the door.

"Come in," Lord Richard said.

They all turned, expecting to see Ellen, back in her maid's uniform and looking innocent as a child caught with her hand in the biscuit tin. Poppy clenched her fists, ready to hear more of Ellen's denials, but it wasn't Ellen who came in.

It was Lydia again, looking triumphant.

"Pardon, Your Lordship, but she won't come," she said with great relish.

"Oh?" Lord Richard merely raised his eyebrows. Poppy opened her mouth, but he gave her a quelling look and she sat back in her chair. "Did she say why?"

"She said that she's injured," Lydia reported, still looking smug. "But she hasn't done a lick of work all night! She disappeared before the ball, and now she's lying under the blankets moaning."

Poppy hopped to her feet. "I'll go see what's amiss."

"Gently, Poppy, please," Lord Richard cautioned. "Just because she has not been very agreeable doesn't mean that she still isn't a victim."

Poppy grimaced. "I know."

"May I come? I shall wait outside her bedroom, of course," Roger said.

"No, no," Lord Richard said. "Please rejoin the other guests, Roger. Poppy will probably do best on her own." He smiled down at Poppy, who grinned back.

She positively flew up the stairs to the little garret room where Ellen slept, and entered without knocking. She had been hoping to catch Ellen up and about, not at all weak or injured, but again was stopped short with surprise.

Ellen was in bed, but she had thrown back the blankets and was clutching one of her feet. She had bitten her lower lip until it bled, and her face was wet with tears.

"What in heaven's name—" Then Poppy caught sight of Ellen's other foot, and couldn't think of what to say next. After a moment she swore one of her brother-in-law Heinrich's choicest oaths, and quickly shut the door behind her.

Ellen opened her eyes for a moment, but then shut them again. She rocked back and forth and whimpered, clearly beyond caring how she looked or who saw her.

And to Poppy's mind, she had good reason to be distressed. Because from the ankle down, Ellen's feet had turned into shining white glass.

Belle

Cold. So cold that it burned.

The paralyzing coldness of her feet was so intense that echoes of it shot up her legs like lightning bolts. Ellen lay on her narrow bed and sobbed, not caring that Poppy was there, staring at her.

How could her godmother have done this to her?

When the Corley first appeared to her—her own magical godmother to protect her and help her—Ellen had been filled with a constant thrill of excitement. At last, her life would finally be put to rights. She could leave servitude behind forever and restore her family's name. Her godmother had promised her all that and more: marriage to a doting and wealthy husband—a prince even! She would soon be the toast of Society, the most beautiful and envied woman in Castleraugh. The promises were all too glorious.

Far too glorious, in fact.

Since her first appearance as Lady Ella on the night of the

royal gala, her godmother would hardly speak to her. In fact, she seemed annoyed when Ellen went to visit her in her glass-pillared palace. She had no time to talk, and when she did it was to scold Ellen for not dancing every dance with Prince Christian.

"But Roger Thwaite is an old friend," Ellen had protested.

"We need to ensnare the prince," the Corley said.

"Ensnare? But why? And if he doesn't fall in love with me—"

"Do not even suggest such a thing, Eleanora," the Corley had retorted. "You will marry Prince Christian, and that is that! Now be off with you. It's late, and you need your rest. You look peaked, and I have already expended my powers quite enough on your behalf without having to work over your face to make it less drawn."

Terrified at what "working over her face" might entail, Ellen had fled. That had been last night, and so it was with great trepidation that she entered the Corley's palace tonight for her toilette. But her godmother was all smiles, and once again she was petted and pampered, massaged and scented.

And then the slippers, again, of glass.

Her feet had not been right since the night of the first gala. The skin had seemed smooth and unyielding, and her toes felt stiff. She tried to shrug it off as lack of dancing practice, and only mentioned it to the Corley when the stiffness hadn't faded by the night of Marianne's ball.

"You should have returned to me before the clock began to strike midnight last time, dear one," the Corley scolded as Ellen

was sewn into the rose and gold gown. "Once you and your handsome prince are married, I will have time to fix your feet. But not now! Now we must get you ready for tonight. Let this serve as a reminder to be home before the clock begins to strike twelve!"

When she saw her godmother approach her with a swirling pan of liquid glass, gleaming like pink roses and gold, she felt sweat break out all over her body. Maids rushed to fan her and apply more rice powder to her damp forehead. She clenched the arms of the chair and didn't make a sound as her godmother shaped the glass.

Taking her mind off what was happening to her feet, she thought about her gown.

She had been praying that she wouldn't be dressed as a richer copy of Poppy again. It had made her feel a bit superior last time, but to keep doing it seemed mean.

But when she saw that she was to be gowned like a more luxurious version of Marianne, she felt her heart sink. Marianne was sweet, if a bit spoiled, and Ellen knew the girl would hate her for stealing away the young men at her birthday ball. It would be worse still to show up in Marianne's own gown.

One look at the Corley's face, however, her matronly smile fixed and her eyes hard, had convinced Ellen not to protest. For the masked ball she would have to be gowned differently from either girl. The whole point of it was to be unique so no one would guess who you were. And Poppy had said that she would not attend at all. Masked balls apparently caused her

even more anxiety than the usual sort, something that Ellen was beginning to understand.

According to rumor, Poppy and her sisters had danced their shoes to shreds every night before the oldest two princesses had married. "Imagine what your feet would feel like if you had to dance every night," she thought. Even without glass slippers it would not be pleasant.

When the Corley was done, Ellen looked down to see the exquisite shoes. They were like flowers of pink crystal and fine gold cupping her feet.

And they hurt more than she could possibly imagine.

The pain had been bearable last time but as the hot glass touched her stiff feet, steam rose up and she felt a cold so intense that it burned. The only bonus was that it seemed to loosen the stiffness in her toes.

Mute servants helped her out of the chair, and she swayed for a moment before regaining her balance. They fussed over her, straightening her hair and dusting rouge onto her pale cheeks, while Ellen fought the dizziness that was threatening to overcome her.

"Drink this," the Corley had said, and handed her a goblet of something that smelled sweet and spicy at the same time.

Ellen drank, and blessed coolness ran down her body and into her feet. She could take a step, then another. The pain was still there, but remote now, and she felt her blood singing.

"Now, go and dance with your prince, my dear," her

godmother had told her with a smile. "Go and dance and dazzle them with your beauty!"

All this Ellen told Poppy, while the princess sat on Lydia's bed in silence. It was a relief to tell someone what was happening, it was a relief to confide her fears that perhaps her godmother was not as kind as she had seemed, and it was a relief that Poppy didn't say anything during the narrative.

But when Ellen finished, Poppy had plenty to say.

"I can't even imagine what you were thinking, agreeing to do the bidding of some creature you had never met before in your life," Poppy said, clucking her tongue.

"But she's my godmother," Ellen protested, bristling.

"How do you know that? Have you seen the christening record? Does it say 'the Corley' under *godmother*? You must have known she wasn't mortal: normal humans don't live in palaces that you enter through piles of ash."

Ellen wanted to argue with this, but she honestly couldn't. She should have been more wary, she should have asked more questions, or at least not been so quick to agree to her godmother's requests.

"But can you really blame me?" She asked the question after a long silence between the two of them, and was embarrassed at how meek and small her voice was. "She was so kind. And everything was so wonderful. The gowns—" She plucked at the coarse wool of her blankets. "The jewels . . ." She closed her eyes and leaned back on the thin pillow, waiting for a mocking comment from Poppy.

None was forthcoming, however.

"Yes, I know why you did it," Poppy said quietly. "But you realize now that you need help, don't you?"

"Yes," Ellen said, her voice still small. "But how? I have to attend the masquerade. I have to marry Prince Christian."

"Oh do you?" Now a snap came to Poppy's voice. "Whether or not *he* wants to marry *you*?"

"I have to," Ellen said again. And then, to her embarrassment, she burst into noisy sobs. Her nose started to run, and she clutched the blankets to her face. "I have to."

If she didn't marry Christian, what would she do? She had to get away from Seadown House, away from being a maid. Away from Castleraugh, where everyone knew her family's shame.

"Stop that at once," Poppy said. But she didn't sound angry, more like uncomfortable. "I have eleven sisters, you know. I don't exactly enjoy watching girlish hysterics." The princess got to her feet. "Besides, blubbing isn't going to get you out of this. But I will!" Poppy headed for the door.

"Where are you going?" Ellen raised her face from the blankets.

"I'm going to tell Roger and Lord Richard everything you've just told me," she said briskly. She opened the door, and they heard the clock strike two. "Oh, blast! No, first I'm going to help Marianne say good-bye to her guests, *then* I'm going to tell Roger and Lord Richard everything you told me." Poppy swept out, breathtaking in her silver and violet gown.

After she was gone, Ellen reflected that, no matter how abrupt and strange the girl could be, Poppy would never

need the Corley's magic to help her snare a prince, or anyone else she wanted. She had the bearing of a princess, through and through, no matter the situation.

More tears leaked out of Ellen's eyes, and she lay back and sniffled. Then she fumbled a handkerchief out from under her pillow and tried to wipe off her face. Poppy had said that Roger was going to help, and she didn't want him to see her looking all red and puffy.

Rejected

Christian felt like he was just waking from a long sleep. Something strange was afoot, but no one would tell him what. Lady Margaret still snapped at everyone, but Marianne was in better spirits and thoroughly enjoyed the rest of her ball. Christian was quite pleased about this, and danced with her twice after Lady Ella left.

But Poppy and Roger were missing, and Marianne would only hint that they were "setting things to rights." Christian just hoped that they weren't planning on doing something to humiliate poor Lady Ella for copying Poppy's and Marianne's gowns. It was rude of her to do it, but she was a nice girl and he didn't want to see her completely undone by her folly.

Especially if he was going to marry her.

The thought stopped him cold.

He was standing near the punch bowl, having a drink with Marianne and a few other friends, and he froze with his glass halfway to his lips. Now where had that sudden conviction come from? He didn't want to get married!

But his head was suddenly filled with visions of Lady Ella meeting his parents, walking down the aisle of the family chapel in a white gown . . . He could picture it all: what he was wearing, what she was wearing, the music that was playing, his little sisters as bridesmaids. What a queer thing!

"Are you all right?" Dickon Thwaite nudged his arm, and Christian slopped punch over his wrist. "Oops, sorry!" Dickon passed him his handkerchief.

"I just had a sudden . . . vision? Daydream?" Christian shook his head. He'd thought the muzziness was leaving him, but here it was back again!

"About whom?" Dickon waggled his eyebrows. "Lady Ella? Of course it was, you sly dog!" He lowered his voice. "And don't think we aren't all having the same daydreams!"

Marianne was standing right next to Christian, talking to another young woman. But she turned at Dickon's words, and Christian braced himself for her to start screaming at the younger Thwaite brother. She, and all the other ladies except Poppy, had been quite volatile about any mention of Lady Ella.

To his horror, however, Marianne's eyes simply filled with tears. "I despise you," she whispered, and ran off.

Christian looked at Dickon with wide eyes, but the other young man merely shrugged. "Can't stand a bit of competition," he said breezily, and poured himself more punch.

"Dickon!" Christian put his own glass down. "You and Marianne . . . I thought . . . everyone thinks . . ." He found

himself struggling to speak past his astonishment. "You were all but betrothed!"

"I? To Marianne? Of course not!" Dickon snorted. Then his genial brown eyes hardened. "Of course, if you would step aside and let a fellow have a chance with Lady Ella . . ."

"Hear, hear!" Another young man stepped up, looking angrily at Christian. "Just because you're a prince doesn't mean you get to steal the prettiest lady in Breton!"

"Exactly." Dickon had put down his glass now, and his fists were clenched.

Christian opened his mouth to ask what on earth had come over the normally light-minded Dickon. Or even perhaps to say diplomatically that there were many pretty Bretoner ladies, which was certainly the truth. But instead he said, "Lady Ella is going to be my wife, and the future queen of the Danelaw!"

He wasn't sure who was more shocked by this statement: himself or his listeners. Dickon's fist connecting with his jaw was almost less of a surprise than his own words.

Christian reeled back, his own fists rising instinctively, and it looked as if the other youth were about to join the fray as well. But there was a rustling of silk and a female voice rose in some foreign oath.

"Stop this at once!" Poppy stepped between Christian and the other two young men. "Or I'll have you dunked into a horse trough to cool off—all three of you!"

Christian put his hand to his jaw, feeling it gingerly. He would have a bruise there, he knew, but didn't think it would

be too swollen. He gave Dickon a rueful look, hoping to at least share their humiliation, but Dickon was still looking at him with hate-filled eyes.

"Dickon Thwaite," Poppy said in a low, dangerous voice. "You will go to Marianne this instant and tell her that she looked stunning, and wish her a happy birthday, and then you will take your leave. If you don't, I will do something so horrible to you that I don't even know the word for it in the Bretoner language."

Dickon blanched and headed for the entrance hall. Poppy swept the room with her indignant gaze. The ball was over, the musicians packing up their instruments, and many of the guests had already left anyway. Under Poppy's baleful eye, everyone cheerfully wished Marianne many happy returns, complimented her gown, and then left with as much haste as their dignity allowed.

Everyone except Christian.

"I think something . . . unnatural is going on," he confided to Poppy as the last of the guests kissed Marianne's hand and bowed to Lady Seadown.

"Of course it is," Poppy said absently. She was already turning toward Lord Richard's study. "But we'll get it sorted out."

"It has to do with Lady Ella, doesn't it?"

She had taken several steps away, and so he raised his voice to ask. Marianne heard and just shook her head, still looking a bit tearful. Lady Margaret scowled and turned away.

"Yes," Poppy said over her shoulder. "But really, it's no good

even telling you until it's all over. Just make sure you keep the bracelet I gave you on all the time. It will protect you." Her voice sounded oddly muffled.

"But do you have one for Lady Ella? I don't want my future bride to be hurt!" Again, it was as though his mouth moved without his permission. A voice in the back of his head was screaming that this wasn't right, but he couldn't force himself to refute the statement.

Marianne gasped, and Poppy's back stiffened. She moved her head so that she no longer looked over her shoulder at him, but straight ahead to the closed door of Lord Richard's study.

"Lady Ella will be taken care of," Poppy said calmly.

"Exactly as she deserves to be," Marianne began with great vehemence. "The horrid little—"

But Poppy put out one hand and took hold of her friend's arm. "Come along, Marianne. Good night, Christian."

"But Poppy!" Christian took a step toward her. "If something's going on, I want to help!"

"I don't think you can," Poppy said, so softly that he almost didn't catch the words. "Good night."

Strategist

The bracelet and the potion are helping Christian, but not enough," Poppy said, her voice tense, when she entered Lord Richard's study. "I'm sorry. It looks like Roger will need to brew more. A great deal more. It's worn off of Dickon again as well." She wished she had her knitting. She'd located more unbleached wool earlier, and she wanted to make Christian another charm.

Lord Richard opened his arms and Marianne went to give her father a hug. "I'm sorry your ball was rather spoiled by all this, my dear."

"It's all right," Marianne said, but she swiped the back of her hand across her eyes. "As long as this ends soon."

Roger Thwaite cleared his throat. "Along those lines, Poppy, were you able to speak with Eleanora?"

Sinking down into one of the large leather chairs first, Poppy heaved a sigh. "Oh yes. She told me everything." She stretched her legs out, wiggling her feet in their satin dancing shoes. "But only because she's rather the worse for wear at this point. Those shoes didn't just look like glass, they *were* glass. Melted onto her feet. If she wore them past midnight they would harden and probably stay on forever. And that's just to begin with." Poppy shook her head, not even sure how to go on.

"But where did she get the shoes?" Roger wanted to know.

"Someone—or possibly some*thing*—called the Corley contacted her," Poppy said. "The Corley claims to be Ellen's godmother. That's who her mysterious patron is. In return, all Ellen has to do is dance with no one but Christian, so that he will fall in love with her and marry her."

Seeing their stares, Poppy allowed herself a small smile. She settled back, waited until Marianne had perched herself on the arm of her father's chair, and then told them the rest. The visits to the palace beyond the ashes, the mute servants, the curfew, everything that Ellen had passed on to her.

"What she doesn't understand, and neither do I," Poppy finished, "is why this Corley is so keen to have her marry Christian." She raised one eyebrow at Lord Richard.

"Yes, Poppy, I will tell you everything I know," he said. "But Eleanora needs to hear it as well, so if she cannot leave her bed, we'll have to join her upstairs."

Out of the corner of her eye, Poppy saw Roger's cheeks turn red at the idea of seeing Ellen in her bedchamber. He was really and truly in love with her, Poppy thought. She hoped that Ellen returned his feelings and was only chasing after Christian because of the Corley's influence. Roger was kind and good, and deserved to have his affection returned.

She got to her feet, and the rest of them followed, but Lady Margaret came in before they could leave the study. She was flushed and looked angry, and Poppy could tell that her mother's elegant cousin was still in high dudgeon over Ella's presence at the ball.

It was Marianne who stepped up to diffuse the situation.

"Oh, Mama! Please don't say anything about Lady Ella!" Marianne sniffled and threw her arms around her mother's neck. "I can't bear to hear any more about her!"

Lady Margaret hugged Marianne, looking almost disappointed. "All right, my love, all right. Shh."

"I'm going to take Marianne up to bed," Poppy said, rising to take Marianne's arm. "It's been such a long day."

"Yes, my dear," Lord Richard said to his wife. "Shall I escort you to our rooms? Thwaite wanted to have a look at some of our Far Eastern art pieces. Thwaite, you go on ahead, and I'll meet you."

And so, with Lord Richard helping his wife, Poppy pretending to help Marianne, and Roger ducking into the parlor to look at some vases there, they made their roundabout way to the top of the house.

Poppy knocked, and when a quavering voice told them to enter they all filed in. Ellen was sitting up in her bed with the blankets folded back from her feet, which gleamed eerily in the candlelight. She looked startled to see them all crowding into her small room, and embarrassed when she saw Roger.

"I'm sorry," she said softly to no one in particular.

"Not at all, my dear," said Lord Richard. He gestured for Poppy and Marianne to sit on the other bed, and leaned back casually against one of the walls. "As young as you are, and in your situation, it is no surprise that you were taken in by the Corley. Older and wiser people than you have made terrible bargains with that creature."

"Oh really?" Eleanora's voice was more bleak than interested.

"Oh yes," Lord Richard said. "People like your father. And myself."

Without even waiting for them to all stop gasping, Lord Richard plunged right into his story.

"I inherited the earldom from my father when I was only twenty-two. I was traveling abroad for a year after university, and I came home to find the old man gone, myself an earl, and a pile of debts I hardly knew what to do with. My father could never resist a business venture; he positively threw money at every ship's captain, explorer, and inventor who darkened his doorway. None of them ever amounted to anything, and he'd come to selling off family heirlooms, furniture, art—all for a fraction of what they were worth—just to send more money to these diamond hunters and steam-engine builders."

Lord Richard shook his head sadly. "I was about to sell the country estate—I had no other choice—and was taking a ride around the grounds one last time. There's a stream that runs into a pool at the bottom of the park, and just as I stopped to water my horse the stream turned green. I started to back away, but then I heard a voice telling me exactly what I wanted to hear: that my fortune was about to change, that I wouldn't have to sell the estate, that I could buy back our heirlooms. This benefactress, called the Corley, would make sure my luck ran high, and with a few hands of cards I would be wealthier than I'd ever dreamed."

There was silence in the room. Lord Richard stared at the worn floorboards, Marianne had her mouth open, Roger looked shocked, and Eleanora's eyes were as round as an owl's.

"What was the catch?" Poppy clasped her hands on her knees. "There's always a catch." She knew this for certain. After all, her mother's bargain with a creature of the underworld had resulted in her bearing twelve girls that the King Under Stone then tried to steal away for his sons to marry.

"The catch? First off, I helped to ruin your father, Eleanora, for which I am sorrier than anything else I have ever done in my life." Lord Richard smiled at the girl, not his usual rakish smile that made him seem years younger, but a hard, grim, sad smile. "When he tried to recover some of his fortune through cards, I was told to play against him over and over again, until he had not a farthing left to his name. And I did, heaven help me."

He coughed uncomfortably and stared over their heads at the wall. "After I'd restored the estate, bought back the things Pa had sold off, I invested some money and looked to get away from the Corley. I was married, we had Marianne, and Margaret didn't like my gambling, you see. For a time I told myself it was all to restore the family name, and then to provide for Margaret and our daughter, but the truth was that I could

have found other ways to make money, could have stopped much sooner.

"I was sick to death with what I had done. I no longer wished to play cards, ever again, and I told the Corley so."

"And she let you go?" Eleanora's soft voice was hopeful.

"Of course not!" A bitter laugh. "She flew into a towering rage! She said that Margaret had ruined me, that we were not fit to raise a child . . ." He closed his eyes and whispered, "And she demanded that I give her Marianne."

"What?" Marianne clutched the iron bedstead, her face white.

"Clearly I refused," Lord Richard said, laying a gentle hand on his daughter's shoulder and giving it a squeeze. "She said that you would be pampered and adored, raised as a princess, and one day be married to a prince."

"Why do these creatures always want to marry somebody off?" It sounded ridiculous as soon as Poppy said it, but she didn't care. She put an arm around Marianne's waist, and discovered that her hands were shaking. Marianne laid her head on Poppy's shoulder, and Poppy straightened, willing herself calm.

"What *is* the Corley?" Roger asked.

"How did you get out of the bargain?" Marianne said a beat later.

"I don't know what the Corley is, a witch or sorceress I suppose," Lord Richard said. "A vicious vindictive creature, whatever she is.

"I got out of the bargain by going to the Church and

admitting what I had done. They sent an army of mages to help me. The rituals went on for days, but at the last I was free of the Corley's hold."

Poppy blew her breath out in a great puff of air. So the Corley's grasp could be loosened. She wasn't as dangerous as Under Stone, then. Some good news at last!

"We'll contact these mages," Roger said decisively. He stepped toward Ellen. "We'll release you from your bargain, and everything will be all right," he told her.

"I've already sent word to Roma," Lord Richard said, but his voice was still bleak.

"Roma?" Poppy looked at him, and their eyes locked. "And by the time they get your letter, and decide what to do, and send aid . . ."

"It might be too late," Lord Richard finished.

"It *will* be too late," Ellen whispered. "Christian must propose to me before he returns to the Danelaw for the holidays. Next week."

Eleanora

Wishing that she had confided in Lord Richard earlier, Ellen found herself being carried downstairs to one of the guest rooms by Roger Thwaite. There she was dressed in a lace-trimmed nightgown and was tucked into bed (by Mrs. Hanks, not Roger, of course), with a hot cup of chocolate at her elbow and the instruction to ring if she needed anything else.

"I blame myself for your family's downfall, Eleanora," Lord Richard announced. He held up a hand to stop her protesting. "Yes, your father's affairs were already in tatters when the Corley set me against him, but I fear I dealt him his deathblow. I will not hear of you working another minute as a servant, from now on you must be our guest, and we will care for you as for our own daughter."

"Thank you," Ellen said, her voice coming out in a sob.

Lord Richard took both her hands and squeezed them, and Marianne gave her a handkerchief and a smile.

"First she wanted Marianne, now she's got her claws into

Ellen," Poppy said, her hands busy knitting something small and pale that looked like a kind of sailor's knot. "And both of them were to marry princes. Why? And would she have married Marianne to Christian? Or would George have done just as well?" She frowned, counted stitches, and then went on knitting.

"Perhaps she's after the Dane navy," Roger said, coming back into the room now that Ellen was decent. "If the future queen of the Danelaw were beholden to her, it would give her quite a bit of power in the mortal world."

"Convenient that Christian is here to dance with Lady Ella, then, isn't it?" Poppy looked at them wryly, but Ellen thought she saw a flicker of something in her eyes. Fear?

"Do you think she's behind that as well?" Marianne's eyes were huge. "Did she make King Rupert invite Christian? How could she get to him?"

"This does seem a bit . . . all-encompassing," Lord Richard said, restlessly adjusting a picture frame. "The fact that she is able to make whole housefuls of people fall in love with Eleanora . . . I don't know what to think . . ." He trailed away, looking pensively at a painting of a deer drinking from some idyllic stream.

Ellen squirmed a little under her pile of blankets. Poppy must have caught the motion, and looked up again from her knitting. Her gaze wasn't fearful now, but thoughtful.

Marianne had been staring at the canopy of Ellen's bed, in much the same way her father was now gazing at the painting of the deer. Ellen wondered if the other girl resented

her: resented her birthday ending with them all fussing around a downtrodden maid who was now wearing one of Marianne's own nightgowns.

But Marianne, as she had several times tonight, surprised Ellen.

"Has the Corley been planning this since Ellen was born?" Marianne's voice was musing. "Did she have Ellen's father ruined so she could control Ellen?

"I wonder, Father, if she went after Ellen as a result of you backing out of the deal." She wrinkled her nose.

A tingling sensation ran through Ellen's body, from the top of her head all the way to her toenails, and she gasped aloud. Everyone looked at her, and she clutched the blankets tighter.

"The ironing ruined," she said, her voice coming out strangled. "Laundry soiled, china broken, hair tangled, silver tarnished! No matter how I tried for years to be a good maid, everything turned out wrong."

She looked up and met Poppy's eyes. She had talked to the princess before about this, and wasn't sure that Poppy had believed her at the time. Now she saw that the other girl did.

"I think she sabotaged my work, but why would my godmother—the Corley, I mean—care if I ruined the sheets?"

"If you'd enjoyed being in service you might not have been as ready to accept her deal," Marianne offered.

The Corley was to blame. And she'd been too caught in her pride and resentment to notice it.

Ellen looked down at the humps and hillocks of the

bedding. Her cheeks were burning, and she didn't dare to meet anyone's eyes.

"I think we should let Eleanora rest," Roger said.

She turned his words over, searching for traces of disgust, of condemnation, but found none. She looked up cautiously, and saw him smiling at her with a line of concern between his level brows.

"We should all get some rest," Lord Richard said. "And tomorrow, we'll start fresh."

They all wished each other good night, and the others filed out. Marianne turned out all the lamps but the one on the bedside table that Ellen could reach.

After they had gone, Ellen snuffed that one as well and lay in the dark, thinking. She had started the day as a maid named Ellen. Had danced at a ball as the most fascinating and yet hated woman in the room, Lady Ella. And now she was going to sleep as a guest of the Seadowns, someone to be respectfully bid good night, watched over and cared for.

Someone named Eleanora.

Prey

Now when she found herself dreaming of being in the Palace Under Stone, Poppy hardly had the energy to be frightened.

Jaded, she wandered the corridors, trailing her fingers along the cold walls and wondering what half-mad pronouncements Rionin and Blathen were going to make tonight. Whenever she encountered them, they swore that she would never leave again, or some such thing. She looked down and saw that she was wearing the violet and silver gown from Marianne's ball, and was quite pleased. It was her new favorite, and she wanted to make sure that Blathen got a good look at what he was missing, even if it was all in her own head.

She was still smiling about this when she came into the ballroom, and saw the usual arrangement: the courtiers dancing to give their king power, while Under Stone and his remaining brothers huddled on the dais. This time, though, there was someone with them. An old woman, crouched like a toad on a velvet-cushioned chair.

"You're the Corley, aren't you?" Poppy went right to the foot of the dais to study the woman.

"So I have been called," the old witch said.

"And Eleanora's godmother, or so you call yourself," Poppy said. "If you want her to attract a princely husband, you might want to avoid maiming her." She wondered if this was really what the Corley looked like, if there was something prophetic in her dreams.

"What business of it is yours?" Blathen pushed his way forward to stand just in front of Poppy. He looked her over and licked his lips.

Giving him a look of deep disgust, Poppy tossed back her hair. "Well, let's see, I keep having all these tedious dreams with you and now her in them, so I'd say it's rather a lot of my business." She pointed rudely at the Corley, glad that her finger didn't shake.

"Tedious?" Again Blathen licked his lips. "Don't you enjoy visiting your true home?"

Poppy snorted, aware that it was something Lady Margaret would never do. But it suited Poppy. "This isn't my true home, and it never will be."

Rionin got up from his throne and crossed to the edge of the dais. He leaned down, bringing his face close to Poppy's. "Before you wake up, allow me to clarify one thing: you may toss your head and stamp your foot all you like, but you cannot fight us.

"Just like Eleanora, you are nothing but prey."

He pushed her away with a finger that seemed to pierce the

center of her chest like an icicle. She fell and fell until she woke with a lurch in her own bed.

The violet and silver gown lay in a shaft of moonlight, and her nightrobe was damp with sweat as always. She lit a lamp and wrote everything that she had seen and heard in her diary, just as she had been doing for the past few weeks. Then she wrapped herself in a shawl and went to sit by the window. She wouldn't be getting any more sleep that night, so she might as well finish another bracelet.

She decided she would prefer that her dreams not come true.

~

At breakfast, Lady Margaret was reluctant to put on the strange bracelet that Poppy offered her. So reluctant, despite her normally gracious attitude toward any gift, that Poppy suspected magical intervention. But in the end Poppy got it fastened around Lady Margaret's upper arm, and was pleased to see the change that began to overcome the older woman.

She still looked confused, however, so Lord Richard offered her a tumbler of Roger's strange potion and convinced her to toss the glass into the fireplace. It was such a dramatic gesture that Poppy had a hard time not shouting, "Cheers!" whenever someone did it.

"Do you realize that Lady Ella is our own Ellen?" Lady Margaret looked around, astonished, to see if anyone else had come to that same conclusion.

"Not Ellen, my dear, Eleanora," her husband corrected her.

And then, with Marianne and Poppy talking over him and one another to make certain no detail was forgotten, they explained the situation.

Poppy braced herself for an explosion when Lady Margaret discovered that her husband had himself made a deal with the Corley in order to recover his fortune. But when he came to that part of the tale, she merely nodded. After all the explaining was done, she appeared only half-surprised.

"Did you know about the Corley?" Poppy asked.

"Not her name, but I suspected that Richard's luck was more than, well, mere luck," Lady Margaret admitted. "I suppose I didn't really want to know the details." She made a face. "Of course, if I'd known that our daughter's future lay on the line as well, I might have intervened sooner."

"You know I would die before I would let either of you come to harm," Lord Richard said. He lifted his wife's hand from the white tablecloth, and kissed her wrist.

Marianne sighed dreamily, and Poppy found herself stifling a similar noise. Imagine being so *cherished*. It was never something she had really thought about, until she had seen her oldest sisters with their husbands, and now Lady Margaret with hers.

She doubted very much that she would have been cherished like that by Prince Blathen.

Thinking of her erstwhile partner from the Midnight Balls, she drew herself up. They needed to solve this problem, and quickly. The masked ball was only days away.

"What should we do about the royal masquerade?" Poppy

picked up her fork and pressed some lines into the tablecloth. "I suppose I need to go now." She winced. It had sounded like torture before there was a curse involved.

"And Dickon still needs a bracelet," said Marianne. "It looks like we have to have both. Roger's given him the potion four times now," she said to her plate of kippers and toast.

"I'm working on it," Poppy assured her. "Also, Roger's trying to find a Far Eastern herbalist he knows. It's possible that he could help us."

But when Roger came to the manor a few hours later, he shook his head in answer to their eager inquiries. The house at the address he had for Lon Qui was empty, and he had left a message with the landlady, though she did not know where her tenant was or how long he would be gone.

"You'd think if this Lon Qui were any good, he would have cured the old bat's warts," said Dickon, who had accompanied his older brother.

"Drink your medicine," Roger said grimly, and poured some sludgy potion out of a flask and into a glass one of the maids brought in.

Dickon shrugged, drank, and threw the glass in the fireplace, the movements well practiced by now.

"And put this on," Poppy said, wrapping a bracelet around his wrist. She couldn't stand the expression on Marianne's face one second longer. Dickon shook himself like a dog and then his gaze went to Marianne.

"I've been making rather a fool of myself, haven't I?" His normally cheerful demeanor was subdued.

"Yes. Are you quite finished doing so?" Marianne's soft voice was tart.

"I hope so," he told her.

"Then you may sit by me while we plan what to do next," she said.

"I hate to say this, Poppy," Roger said. "But I'm not convinced that your knitted charms are that efficacious. It seems to take the potion as well to make any difference. And even that wears off." He frowned at Dickon.

"Roger," Poppy said evenly, without looking up. "As the knitting doesn't do any harm, either, I will continue to knit these things and tie them on people until the Corley and her glass slippers are just a memory. And that is all I will say about it."

Roger stopped pacing to look at her, then resumed. "Very well, I understand," was all he said.

Poppy didn't think he truly understood—but then, he was the one pacing. She had to keep her hands moving, she had to be doing something, something to help, or she would run mad. If she knit a thousand charms and none of them did a thing, at least she could say that she tried.

Lord and Lady Seadown came in, looking subdued. They had been talking with Eleanora for the last hour, and Poppy saw that Lady Margaret had been crying.

"The poor girl," she murmured, and sank down beside Poppy.

"Eleanora is in no condition to attend the masked ball," Lord Richard announced. "Her feet . . . the skin . . ."

"Her feet are turning to glass!" Lady Margaret cried out as she sank onto the sofa beside Poppy. "Glass, the poor child! The physician has never seen anything like it. He's not sure if it can ever be cured. How could it be? We need to get rid of that Corley creature, and find someone to heal Eleanora."

"Don't worry, Cousin Margaret," Poppy said, knitting even faster. "If it cannot be done in Breton, I'll take her to Westfalin. Galen can help her, and if he can't, we'll find someone who can."

Poppy, who had once shunned Ellen as irritating and depressing, now wanted to help her just as much as she wanted to free Christian from his infatuation with Lady Ella. She had realized in the night that she and Eleanora were really quite similar: their parents had made horrible mistakes, and the children were forced to pay the price.

"What will happen if Eleanora doesn't dance?" Poppy's voice was much more tense than she would have liked. There had been penalties for her and her sisters if they didn't attend the Midnight Balls, even if their absence had not been by their choice.

"I don't know, but the Corley's plans seem to hinge upon the masquerade," Roger said gravely. "Christian will soon return to the Danelaw, and the Corley told Eleanora that the prince must propose to her by the end of the ball."

"But if she doesn't go," Marianne said eagerly, "then he can't propose and the Corley's plan will be ruined!"

"I fear it won't be so easy, my dear," her father said. "The Corley will likely find some way to force her to attend, even if

it cripples her, or she will exact her revenge upon Eleanora for failing."

"It's best to let these things play out," Poppy said, striving to sound knowledgeable but coming out anxious instead. "There's always a chance for escape, but you have to wait for just the right moment."

She thought of the last night she had spent in the Palace Under Stone, not in a dream, but in reality. She thought of dancing at the ball with one eye on her sister Rose, who had tried to make a bargain of her own before Galen had helped them escape. The scream from the King Under Stone as Galen's silver knitting needle pierced his heart would haunt her for the rest of her life, but the sense of lightness, of freedom, that she had felt when she ascended the golden stair for the last time was worth the occasional nightmare.

"But in order to let this play out," Roger argued, "Eleanora will have to attend the masked ball."

"Not necessarily," Poppy said suddenly. "It's a *masked* ball. Someone wearing glass slippers will have to attend, and be proposed to by Christian." Her eyes met Marianne's, and the color drained from the other girl's face.

"I—I—I couldn't possibly! No!" Marianne clutched at Dickon, who put his arm around her.

"Out of the question," Dickon said. "I'm not letting Marianne risk her life standing in as a decoy!"

"It's all right, Marianne, I'll do it," Poppy said. "I'm more of a height with Eleanora anyway. No one will even know the difference."

She looked back at her knitting as though the decision were only of passing importance. On the mantel, the clock ticked loudly as everyone else in the room stared at her, in admiration, in horror, in speculation.

Despite her nonchalance, in her head Poppy kept hearing the voice of the King Under Stone: "You are prey."

Confused

Wandering from room to room in Tuckington Palace, Christian did his best to stay out of the way of the bustling servants. The weather had turned stormy, with great gales of wind and torrents of rain pouring down, preventing him from riding. Even Hermione and Emmeline were too busy with the fittings for their costumes to plague him.

But the entire palace was taken up in preparations for the masked ball. All the bedrooms were being aired out, floors were scrubbed and waxed, laundry boiled and hung to dry indoors so that the servants' quarters and kitchens looked like an army camp with pristine white tents every two paces. The kitchen servants wove in and out around the sheets and towels with expert skill, whisking and baking and icing thousands of little cakes, bonbons, and other delicacies for the refreshments. The regular meals suffered because of it, and Christian had made a solemn vow that if he was served cold meat pie one more time he was going to start taking all his meals at the nearest pub, and never mind the proprieties.

After finding himself yet again halfway down a hallway he didn't recognize, and unable to think what he was doing there, Christian finally just went back to his room. He started a letter to his parents, tore it up, started a letter to his sisters, and tore that up as well. There were green sparkles in the corners of his eyes again, and his head throbbed. The bracelet Poppy had given him itched worse than anything he had ever worn, yet he didn't want to take it off.

Poppy had made it, just for him, as a sign of friendship . . . or something more? The letter to his parents that he had just cast into the fireplace had started out as a request that Poppy be invited to Damerhavn after her visit to Breton was over. He'd discarded it because he didn't know how to describe his feelings about Poppy to his parents . . . or to himself. Were they just friends? Or did he care more deeply for her? What did she feel for him? He hoped that spending time with her in his home, with his family, would help him understand.

But Ella will be there, a little voice nagged in his head. *And she might not like having Poppy around.*

Christian frowned and shook his head. Ella? Why would Lady Ella be there? She wasn't a pawn in this grand marital game, like himself and Poppy.

His cheeks went hot at the idea of introducing Poppy to his family as a potential bride. He imagined her riding through the streets beside him, though, still awkward on horseback but

determined not to show it. And she would love the Danelaw: it was very near to Westfalin and she could visit her family. Perhaps he would get to meet them as well.

There was a sudden zing through his body, as though he had been struck by lightning, and hot guilt poured over him. How could he have been thinking of courting Poppy? He hoped that Lady Ella, his darling intended, never found out about his treacherous thoughts!

Christian shook his head again, feeling the fog come back. Lady Ella? He knew nothing about her! His parents would have to meet her, and he wouldn't invite a girl to travel all the way to his home before he had met her parents . . . or guardian, in Lady Ella's case. She had never said, but he got the impression that she was an orphan. There was a mysterious godmother that she made reference to. And those references were mysterious indeed. Even King Rupert, with his determination to see Christian married to a Bretoner lady, could find out nothing about Lady Ella.

"For all we know, she's a pirate or a laundress who has stolen someone else's gowns," Christian muttered aloud.

Instantly another zing of lightning coursed through him, this one powerful enough to make him cry out. The throbbing in his head became a blinding pain that settled behind his right eye and sent him reeling to his bed. He flung himself across the mattress, clutching at his head with one hand. The bracelet Poppy had given him itched so fiercely now that it felt like his wrist was on fire. One of these pains had to go away, or he would end up barking mad!

He started to rip the bracelet off, but stopped himself just in time. Through the green sparkles that kept sending him visions of Lady Ella dancing in her glowing slippers, he saw glimmers of Poppy in her red and white gown from the gala.

Poppy, with her regal bearing and flashing eyes. Poppy gambling like a hardened cardsharp and teasing Roger Thwaite about his stern demeanor. Poppy in lavender, with her knitting needles flashing and the tip of her tongue in the corner of her mouth—a habit she denied.

She had put this bracelet on him for a reason.

He took his hand away from his head, and forced himself to breathe deeply in and out. He clutched at the bracelet, not to tear it away, but to press the wool even tighter against his skin. He raised his shaking hands and rubbed the itchy band against his forehead, against his eyelids.

The green sparkles fled and the pain subsided.

Still holding his wrist to his forehead, Christian got to his feet. He needed to see Poppy right away; it seemed that the bracelet she had made for him had some sort of power. But why? To prevent headaches? Or was it a love charm, to entice him?

He snorted at the very idea. Poppy wouldn't try to ensnare him with some love charm!

Scrubbing his forehead with the rough wool bracelet, he lurched for the bedroom door. He had to get to Seadown House; from there he could send for Roger as well. Roger knew things; Roger would help.

He fumbled the door open and nearly bowled over a small

man with ridiculously curled hair and an elaborate green waistcoat that made Christian's eyes sting. It reminded him of the green sparkles, and he had to look away quickly before they returned.

"Your Highness!" The man bowed with much flourishing of lace cuffs.

"Who are you?"

"Monsieur Flamonde," the little man said. "The tailor!" More flourishing. "Your Highness's costume is ready to be fitted!"

"Costume?" Christian sagged weakly against the doorframe.

King Rupert came stumping along the passageway. "Flamonde, you must do our guest right!" He slapped the small man on the back, nearly pitching the tailor into Christian's arms. "There may be an announcement after the unmasking, and Prince Christian will want to look his best!" King Rupert winked and chortled through his mustache, and Christian felt even more ill.

"An announcement! Will there be wedding clothes ordered soon?" The tailor rose up on his toes in excitement, which did not add much to his height. In fact, he was already wearing shoes with heels almost too high to be masculine, and still barely came to Christian's chin.

"Very soon," King Rupert said.

"I'm going to ask Lady Ella," Christian said, hearing his voice as if from a great distance, "Lady Ella to—to marr—"

His head throbbed, the sparkles returned, the wool band itched, and Christian reeled back into his bedroom. He barely

grabbed the chamber pot in time, retching into the freshly scrubbed porcelain.

"Oh no, Your Highness," Monsieur Flamonde trilled in dismay.

"Prince Christian, what's all this, then?" King Rupert demanded.

Christian almost burst into hysterical laughter. Instead he wiped his mouth on a handkerchief and lurched out of the palace.

He didn't bother to call for a carriage. He just stumbled down the street until he saw a hackney cab. It nearly ran him down, in fact. He flung himself into it, ignoring the driver's cursing and brandishing of the whip, and yelled for the man to take him to Seadown House as quickly as possible.

When they reached the Seadowns' front gate, the driver climbed down, grabbed Christian by the coat collar, and unceremoniously dumped him on the pavement. Christian reached into his pockets, searching for some money, but the man just rolled his eyes.

"Jus' doan get in my cab again, yer daft drunk!" He climbed back onto the cab and sent the horse off at a trot.

Christian staggered through the gate and up the drive. The butler was so shocked by the prince's appearance that he let him inside without a word, pointing toward the drawing room.

Christian managed to get himself through the drawing room door before collapsing. Looking up in a daze, he saw the Seadowns, Poppy, Roger, Marianne, and Dickon all staring down at him.

"What's happening to me?"

"Two might do it," Poppy said enigmatically. She plucked a bracelet from her work basket and tied it around Christian's other wrist. "And Roger, another glassful of that horrid stuff, please."

Dickon propped Christian up and Roger poured something foul down his throat, then guided his hand to break the glass on the hearthstones. Christian could only retch and mumble in response.

Then the green sparkles subsided, and so did the throbbing in his head.

"You're in trouble, my lad," Lord Richard told him when his vision cleared. "A creature known as the Corley has you in her sights."

Christian sat up and stared at His Lordship.

"We're doing our best to stop her," Roger Thwaite said, his voice lower than Lord Richard's. He helped Christian off the floor and onto a chair.

"Oh, good," Christian mumbled.

Then he fainted. Again.

Invalid

But what if she discovers Poppy?" Eleanora sank a little deeper into the pillows of her bed. "She'll be so angry!"

Her voice was little more than a whisper. She wanted to be brave, but lying in bed and hearing horrifying tales about the Corley had made her pray she would never see her "godmother" again.

In an effort to make her feel less useless, Roger had brought her several dusty old books he had discovered that told about the Corley—who she had been and why she had been banished to her strange glass palace. Eleanora had read them with sickening fascination, and now wished she hadn't. Now she knew why the Corley wanted her, or Marianne. And now she knew what lengths the Corley would go to get what she wanted.

The Corley had once been a woman named Mary Bright, the wife of a famous naval captain back in the time of Great Queen Bethune. Her husband, the celebrated Captain Bright, had chased the Spanian pirates from Bretoner waters and been knighted as a reward. But when the Danes had attacked shortly after that, Captain Bright had changed sides and gone to command the Dane fleet, leaving behind his wife.

Instead Captain Bright had taken his "lucky charm" with him: his goddaughter, Mary Bess Corley. Mary Bess's parents had died when she was only two, and the Brights had raised her as their own. Captain Bright had even named his ship *The Corley* in honor of her and her late parents, and never put to sea without his goddaughter's blessing. But Mary Bess had fallen in love with the Crown Prince of the Danelaw, and King Haakon had promised that she would marry his son if Captain Bright would engineer Breton's downfall.

Driven to madness by her husband's betrayal and abandonment, Mary Bright had turned to magic. The daughter of a glassblower and a village wisewoman, Mary conjured a ship of glass, crewed by mute glass sailors, and sent it after her husband's ship. The glass ship rammed *The Corley* and shattered its oak beams into a thousand splinters, sending Captain Bright, his crew, and Mary Bess to the bottom of the sea. Mary Bright, known thereafter as The Corley, vanished.

"She's trying to replace her goddaughter," Poppy said without looking up. She was knitting another charm.

"Do you really think . . . ?" Eleanora blinked.

"I really do," Poppy said. "She wants her goddaughter alive and married to a prince of the Danelaw. She's trying to erase her mistake."

"But that won't . . . I mean, she knows that I'm not *her*, doesn't she?"

Poppy shrugged. "Who can say?" She stopped knitting, unraveled a few stitches, and started up again.

Eleanora was filled with a sudden horror: she would never be free of the Corley! Even if she wasn't called upon to dance at the masked ball, even if the substitution of Poppy worked, the Corley would still chase after her.

"Don't worry," Poppy said. "We will fight, and we will win." Her needles clicked together and the yarn slid through her fingers.

"How can you just sit there and knit?" Eleanora pulled herself up in the bed, her breath coming fast. "How can you just sit there at all? We might be killed!"

"I have to," Poppy said levelly.

"What do you mean, you have to? No one is holding a knife to your throat, forcing you to knit those things!"

Poppy stopped knitting.

She set the yarn and needles on the little table by her chair, folded her hands in her lap, and looked at Eleanora with her large violet eyes.

"I have to keep knitting," she said in low voice. "Because I'm the strong one." And then her eyes filled with tears, and Eleanora watched in helpless shock as Princess Poppy of Westfalin sobbed like a child.

"I'm the strong one," she sobbed. "The tough one. Everyone says so. I'm not like Daisy, I'm not like Lily, I'm not gentle

and sweet and ladylike. My father says it, everyone says it. When we had to dance, at the end, every night and we were so tired and sick I heard Papa saying to the doctor, 'Ask them, Hans, see if they'll tell you what's happening. But don't bother with Poppy. She'll never crack, she's as tough as an old boot.'

"And I was. I never cried, I never gave up. I did what Rose and Galen said, and I never cried. But I thought it was over, I didn't think I would have to do this again, to face something like this. Without my sisters, without my father and Walter and Galen to protect me. I can't play cards against the Corley, I can't swear her to death, so I have to knit. There's nothing else I can do."

"You can dance," said a voice from the doorway.

Both girls turned, and saw Prince Christian standing there, his gaze fixed on Poppy. Seeing the intensity of his eyes on Poppy's tear-streaked face, Eleanora knew that the prince could never have loved Lady Ella the way he loved Poppy, and she wondered if Poppy knew.

"You can dance as Lady Ella," the prince said, coming the way into the room and taking Poppy's hands. "Dance with me. And before the clock strikes midnight, we will defeat her."

"Blast," Poppy said shakily. "It would have to be dancing. I really was hoping to challenge her to a game of cards."

Eleanora laughed out loud.

Replacement

Hands shaking, Poppy poured water over the fire she had built in the parlor grate. She uttered the words that Eleanora had taught her, and waited. She wondered if the rhyme would work, since the Corley was not, in fact, Poppy's "dear godmother." Behind her, she heard tense breathing and rustling clothing, but she shut her ears and said it again.

"Cinders, cinders, smoke and water, take me to my dear godmother!"

The mantel arched up, and what had been a fireplace became a passageway.

Everyone in the room took a step backward, and Poppy trod on Dickon's toes. She blurted out an apology, straightened her spine, and took a firmer grip on her pistol. She was holding it at her side, with a shawl draped across her shoulders to hide the weapon. She didn't know how much good it would do against an immortal creature like the Corley, but its weight comforted her all the same.

"I should go with you," Lord Richard said.

"We've already discussed it, my lord," Roger said. "You were ensnared by her once before; you shouldn't expose yourself again."

Poppy felt the silver dagger beneath her gown. She could get off one shot with the pistol, drop it, and draw the dagger in less than thirty seconds.

She'd been practicing.

No one said anything as she stepped onto the hearth and over the grate, ducking her head even though the entranceway was high enough that even Roger wouldn't have needed to stoop. Soot sifted down onto her hair and clothes, and Poppy reminded herself to apologize to Eleanora later. It seemed clear now that the other girl hadn't put soot on Poppy's linens deliberately.

"Good luck!" Marianne's voice echoed and Poppy waved her left hand by way of acknowledgment, without turning around.

Once past the fireplace and into the hallways of the Corley's palace, the soot and marble were replaced by tinkling glass ornaments and hard, slick floors. Delicate pillars, also made of glass, lined the passageway, and the light was provided by candles in round golden orbs.

"This is certainly more elegant than Under Stone's palace," Poppy said aloud. "Everything there was black or purple, and always seemed a bit tatty." She ran a hand along the smooth walls. "The silver gilt was peeling from the furniture, I swear."

She continued to drag her left hand along the smooth wall

with a casual air. She was glad that the long stole around her shoulders hid the pistol from view. That way no one could see how white her knuckles were. A trickle of sweat ran down her back, and she was fighting the urge to turn and run back to the safety of Seadown House.

"But it isn't safe there," she murmured. "Nothing is safe."

She turned down the corridor and entered the great hall. It was filled with people, silent, slick-skinned people, standing in ranks and staring at her. Poppy muttered a startled oath.

"I'm here," she said a moment later, forcing herself to sound bright and innocuous. "Tonight is the masked ball! See, I already have a costume!"

She twirled so they could see the gown she wore. She was dressed as a Spanian dancer in a purple and scarlet gown with a black mask fitted over the upper half of her face. The Corley would have another costume prepared, of course, but Poppy hoped to keep the mask on, to keep up the ruse that she was Eleanora.

Without hurrying, without even making any noise, the silent servants surrounded Poppy. They didn't touch her, much to her relief, she was afraid she would start screaming if they did, but they turned as one and quickstepped out of the great hall and down a long corridor, herding her along in their midst.

~

Sitting bolt upright on a bench in the enormous bath, Poppy suddenly wished she *had* brought someone with her. She had never faced this type of thing by herself before. The last time

she had been trapped in an otherworldly palace—the Palace Under Stone—all her sisters had been with her.

Of course, she wasn't exactly alone.

She was, in point of fact, surrounded.

A dozen or so of the Corley's mute handmaidens were in the bathroom with her, lying in wait. As soon as she twitched a finger, they would leap forward to offer her a towel, scented soap, a glass of lemonade. Poppy had refused their offers to bathe her like a baby, and now she was at the far end of the tub, soap in one hand, eyes on the servants, wondering if they would try to scrub her back the moment she began to lather.

Finally she took a deep breath, closed her eyes, and washed herself as quickly as she could. She scrubbed her hair and face so fast that she pulled several hairs out and nearly put a finger up her own nose, but at least she was out of the tub quickly. She grudgingly allowed the servants to wrap her in towels and help her onto a padded bench, where they greased her up with various lotions and combed out her wet hair. She kept her face pressed into the bench as much as she could, alert to every sound, in case the Corley should come to check on her beloved goddaughter, but she hadn't so far.

Then the servants led her to a dressing room bursting with fabulous gowns. The sight of them irritated Poppy more than anything: they were just there to taunt Eleanora! Where and when would she ever wear them? The girl had only worn two gowns so far, both of them copies of someone else's finery.

Poppy glared at the gowns all while she was being dressed in

peacock blue satin. There was a great fan of peacock feathers standing behind her head, and feathers trailed from her sleeves and skirt. When she was finally laced and tucked into the gown, she looked at herself in the multiple mirrors and made a face of disgust.

"What a ridiculous gown," she remarked, even though she knew none of the servants would—or could—answer. "How precisely am I supposed to dance with anyone?"

"You aren't supposed to dance with *anyone*," the Corley said. "You are supposed to dance with Prince Christian!"

Poppy snatched the feathered mask from the dressing table and held it to her face. The mask that matched the peacock gown covered even more of her face than the one she had brought. Now if she could just keep her eyes down and her Westfalian accent in check.

"You look so beautiful, my dear," the Corley simpered. "Like a princess . . . no, a queen!" The old witch put her hands on Poppy's shoulders and smiled at her in the mirror, her mouth stretching wider than a human mouth should have been able to.

Poppy shuddered and kept her attention on the maid applying her cosmetics. There was gold and green powder around her eyes already, making them look more blue than violet. Now rouge was added to her cheeks and lips, and a design of green and gilt that curled up the left side of her face from her jaw to her cheekbone. It looked like a peacock's plume, and Poppy found it pleasingly exotic.

Her hair was fastened high with gold combs that sported

more plumes, and the blue feathered mask tied in place with a ribbon that was hidden in her hair.

"Come, my darling! It's time for the final touch!"

Poppy tried not to shiver as she walked barefoot down the passageway in the Corley's wake, to a chamber that smelled of magic and strangeness, and sat down in a large chair with an attached footrest. On a table to the side were bubbling pots of thick liquids, and Poppy broke out in a cold sweat. She thought of Eleanora's feet and reminded herself that it would only be for one night, and Christian and the others would help her.

Unclenching her hands from the armrests, she sat up straight and watched the Corley with her face impassive. She was a princess, after all, and refused to give this creature the satisfaction of seeing her flinch. It helped that a mask hid the upper part of her face and shadowed her eyes, however.

The Corley swept aside Poppy's abundant skirts to expose her bare feet. She snapped her fingers, and a servant brought her a shallow pan of molten blue glass.

The Corley looked directly into Poppy's eyes and without saying a word poured the boiling glass over the girl's feet.

Emperor

Wigs itched, Christian was discovering. His emperor's costume was topped with a long black wig, and it felt like a hot compress draped across his head. But even worse than the warmth was the itching along the edges where the mesh foundation of the abominable thing touched his face and neck, and it was held in place with clips that jabbed his scalp.

Were it not for the wig, the costume otherwise would have been very comfortable, since it was rather like a loose dressing gown of silk over billowing trousers. Even the pointed slippers were light and flexible, and the heavy ivory-and-silk fan that hung from his waist was much more manageable than the cumbersome fake swords that many of the other gentlemen wore.

He had already turned down several offers to dance with various young women. King Rupert, unsubtly dressed as his ancestor, Horcha the Magnificent, smiled benignly at this from his position on the dais at the far end of the ballroom.

He was looking forward to announcing Christian's betrothal after the unmasking at midnight, and no longer felt the need to throw every young lady in Breton at Christian.

For his part, Christian felt like a clock that had been wound too tight. At any moment he feared he might spring to the dais and start screaming at all the smiling, laughing courtiers. Poppy was in danger, they were all under a spell, how could they just drink and dance as though nothing were amiss?

Princess Emmeline twirled by, dressed like a milkmaid (albeit a milkmaid in a satin gown), and Christian fought down a surge of dislike. He remembered her derision about her former maid's clumsiness, which Eleanora now suspected had been caused by the Corley. The poor girl had been orphaned, thrown into the streets, and then slowly drawn into a witch's clutches. All Emmeline ever had to worry about was convincing her parents to let her stay up late to attend a ball, as she was tonight.

And here Christian was, pretending to have no interest in any woman but Lady Ella. Well, it was partially true: he wasn't interested in anyone else. But the majority of his interest came from the fact that Poppy would be Lady Ella tonight.

Would the Corley uncover their deception, and what would happen to Poppy if she did? If she didn't, would Poppy's feet be all right? They still weren't sure if Eleanora could be healed.

And would Poppy really dance all night with him?

Christian kept turning to look at the door of the ballroom but didn't expect Poppy to arrive any time soon. After all, Lady

Ella always appeared late and made a grand entrance, and the masked ball had only been underway for half an hour. Most of the guests had arrived with unusual punctuality, and were also craning their necks around. He suspected that they, too, were waiting for the mysterious Lady Ella, since she had captivated not only Christian, but all the noblemen of Castleraugh, even as she alienated the women.

He wondered if the spell would be broken tonight. Would all the nobles of Castleraugh be talking about Lady Ella to their grandchildren? Or would the magic fade once the Corley had what she wanted?

Or better, once they stopped her.

Christian was drawn from his thoughts by the hush that fell over the ballroom. It was Lady Ella; the guests wouldn't be so quiet for any other reason. He turned to face the double doors and saw a magnificent figure framed there. All in peacock blue silk with plumes of that very bird rising around her head and trailing from her skirts, Poppy looked magnificent.

And there was no doubt in Christian's mind that it was Poppy. No one, he thought, could mistake that proud bearing or sheer vibrancy of spirit. No mask or glamour could hide the fluid grace that said she was a born dancer, for all her professed hatred of dancing. And he couldn't help noticing that her hair was darker and glossier than Ellen's, and her figure? Well, Poppy had a very nice figure.

It wasn't hard to push the other gentlemen out of his way to reach her side first. It wasn't hard to bow and kiss her fingers,

and it was without any compulsion at all that Christian asked her to dance.

A small mischievous smile curled Poppy's lips.

"I would be honored, Your Highness," she said, and slapped his arm with her peacock feather fan.

Christian laughed and took her arm, steering clear of the fan. "*Can* you dance?" He teased as they took their places on the polished floor among a host of dashing pirates and romantic beggar maids. "Or are you merely fond of the occasional entrechat?"

"I have some meager skill," she said airily.

The orchestra began to play a gigue, one of Analousia's more intricate dances, which did make use of the entrechat. Two steps to the left, and Poppy twirled up and down in Christian's arms flawlessly. A woman nearby stumbled, either from clumsiness or because of her elaborate costume, and Poppy skipped lightly out of the way.

Christian marveled that Poppy claimed she hadn't danced in nearly three years. She was the most skilled partner he had ever had, as light in his arms as a butterfly, while carrying on a conversation as easily as though they were seated in the Seadowns' parlor.

Laughing at his expression of amazement, Poppy said, "You must understand: for ten years I danced nearly every night till dawn. You should have seen my feet: blisters, bruises, horrifying. But eventually they healed." Then she made a face. "They're feeling rather delicate now, though."

When they came to the end of the dance, she swept aside her skirts a little, to show him why.

Her gleaming blue shoes were a thing of great beauty. There were swirls of green, and an overlay of gold filigree, all of it made of glass. She wore no stockings, and the blue and gold and green stood out starkly against her pale skin.

"They hurt like nothing you have ever felt," Poppy said fervently, dropping her skirts. "I think I'd rather be run through with a rusty cavalry saber."

Wincing with sympathy, he took her hands and led her into the next dance. They would have to dance every dance, lest the Corley suspect that something was amiss.

"So what do we do now?" Christian wanted to relax and enjoy dancing with Poppy, but he couldn't help but worry about what was coming next. "Do we just wait for the end of the evening? Am I supposed to propose to you?" This last idea did not seem all that repellent, actually.

He noticed that he was not experiencing any of the fogginess, the twisting of his thoughts, that he had had with Eleanora as Ella. Was it the potion and the charms at work? Or was it because it was Poppy wearing the glass slippers?

"I suppose," Poppy said shortly. She had a funny look on her face, but it might have been the mask. "I have to leave before midnight, so we'll do it sometime before then. Roger and all three of the Seadowns are armed with charms and what have you, waiting for the Corley's next move."

Her voice was breezy, confident, but Christian thought he

could detect a slight tremble to it, and saw her chin pucker. He held her a little more closely than the dance demanded, and felt her lean into him.

"Did I ever tell you that the first time my sister Rose danced with her husband Galen, he was invisible?" Poppy's voice was hardly more than a whisper.

"Invisible?"

"He had a cape that made him invisible. That's how he was following us down to the King Under Stone's palace," she said. "He stabbed the king with a knitting needle."

Christian let out a quick laugh. "Is that all we need? One of your knitting needles? The Corley will be gone, poof?"

"Wouldn't that be nice?" she said, laughing breathlessly.

"I wish I was able to do more," Christian said, voicing his frustration.

"Don't you worry," she told him. "Roger has a knife for you, almost a short sword, forged out of blessed silver."

Christian felt relieved: they were going to need him after all. He was good with swords and knives. He rather wished Roger could have located him a rapier, but he imagined that the Corley didn't follow the gentlemanly rules of fencing.

No, better to hack and slash with a sturdy (and magical) short sword than prance back and forth with a needle-thin foil.

"See, Roger is signaling us now," Poppy said. "Let's dance over that way, and get your weapon." She gave a little sigh. "I have one, but it's not half as impressive."

Christian couldn't help laughing as he guided their steps toward a severe-looking figure in judge's robes with a noose tied

to his waist. For one thing, it was just like Roger Thwaite to dress as a "hanging judge" while everyone else was romantically garbed as pirates or knights, and for another, it was just like Poppy to be jealous that her weapon was smaller.

"I shall buy you a short sword for your birthday," Christian promised.

"I'll hold you to that," Poppy said.

"Who is this mysterious lady?" Roger stopped them at the edge of the dance floor and kissed Poppy's hand.

"Oh, sir! Don't tempt me to reveal myself," Poppy simpered, and slapped Roger's arm with her peacock feather fan, shedding a plume.

Christian stifled a snicker at her impersonation of Lady Ella. He'd had a chance to speak to the real Eleanora yesterday, and thought she was a delightful, shy young woman. He had no idea why being Lady Ella made her slap people and pout all the time.

"If you continue to dominate this lovely lady's dance card," Roger said to Christian, "I may have to call you out!" He flapped his robes with uncharacteristic drama, which allowed him to pull out a long knife in a black sheath and press it into Christian's waiting hand.

Christian quickly concealed the knife in the folds of his own robes, not sure what to do with it now. He couldn't very well dance with one hand clamped to his side. He saw Poppy and Roger purse their lips, as though coming to the same conclusion.

A young woman dressed as a hareem girl in a daring costume

of billowing trousers and a low-cut, tight bodice came fluttering over to them. She even had delicate gold shackles on her wrists, Christian noticed, and was further distracted by the fact that her bodice and trousers did not quite meet over her waist. Poppy jabbed him in the ribs with the handle of her fan when she caught him staring.

"Costumes are so difficult to manage, aren't they?"

The hareem girl, to Christian's shock, was Marianne. Her brown eyes twinkled from behind her spangled mask, and her black hair was covered by a headdress dripping with cut-glass "jewels." He swallowed and nodded, still taken aback by the amount of flesh she was showing.

With a laugh at his discomfiture, Marianne took the long knife from his hand and tucked the sheath through the sash of his imperial robes. She tugged at the knot of the sash, making sure it was tight enough, and then gave a satisfied nod.

"You would have to wear the full regalia!" Her voice was louder now, for the benefit of those watching the little group. "I don't know how you expect to dance with all these fans and things hanging off of your sash!"

"Oh, thank you! How kind!" Poppy fluttered her fan at Marianne. "Now if you don't mind!" She steered Christian back onto the dance floor as though jealous.

"Her costume," Christian said in a strangled voice.

"The original design called for one of those long veils, all the way to the floor. But then she decided this morning that it would get in the way when she danced." Poppy gave

a wicked laugh. "Have you seen Dickon? He's dressed to match."

"No, I—" Then Christian stopped, because he did see Dickon, or he assumed it was Dickon, taking Marianne's hand to lead her into a dance.

In complete contrast to his brother's restrained garb, Dickon Twaite was wearing a pair of billowing trousers like Marianne's, a sash with a long knife, a turban, and a mask.

And nothing else.

Christian let out a low whistle.

"Lord Richard is dressed like a cavalier," Poppy said.

At first this seemed to be a rather off-the-cuff remark, but then Christian noticed the tall Analousian cavalier lurking to the side of the dance floor, his masked gaze clearly on Marianne and Dickon. Christian started to laugh, and found that he couldn't stop.

It infected Poppy, too, and soon they were both laughing like maniacs as they twirled around the floor. It was all too surreal: the Corley, Eleanora, the glass slippers . . . and here was Lord Richard worried about the fact that his daughter was wearing a revealing costume and dancing with the young man who was on the verge of asking for her hand anyway.

For hours they laughed and danced, and pretended that there was nothing more horrible to come than the end of the ball.

Christian wondered how he could ever have thought about asking Lady Ella to marry him. Not with Poppy in the same

room, even in the same city. She was clever, and witty, and without a doubt the finest dancer he had ever partnered. Eleanora's awkward flirting, fan-slaps, and stilted conversation simply could not hold a candle to Poppy's free and easy manners.

Of course Christian knew that it was hardly Eleanora's fault. She hadn't had a happy life, and she had no experience with balls and parties. There was also the small matter of her being in love with Roger, while trying to attract Christian's interest on the Corley's orders.

Poppy filled him in on all this as they danced, including her suspicion that Roger would have eloped with Eleanora if he weren't so honorable.

"As it is, I still think he might. If we don't defeat the Corley tonight . . ." She trailed off briefly, then shook herself. "He may just take her and run for it anyway."

"I can't believe that Roger Thwaite could do something so wild," Christian argued. "Of course, I can't believe that Roger could have a childhood sweetheart, either. Dickon yes, but Roger?"

"Well, they both do. So perhaps it's a family trait," Poppy said. "Dickon and Marianne really should be married with all possible speed. Look at them!"

They both twisted to look as they skipped through the steps of the current dance. Dickon and Marianne were trying to stay as close as possible, gazing into each other's eyes like they had never seen anyone so fascinating, and all while they were involved in one of the more intricate Venezian *caribas*.

"They're going to trip," Christian agreed.

"And so is everyone around them, if they don't start—"

But Poppy never finished her thought.

The enormous clock at the far end of the ballroom began to toll the hour: eleven.

"Oh," Poppy's voice was barely a whisper. "I suppose now we should . . . you will have to . . ."

"Er, yes." Christian took her arm and they eased themselves out of the pattern of the dance, through the glass doors at the end of the ballroom, and onto the veranda.

Poppy leaned against the stone balustrade, her face unreadable behind her mask. The moon was full, and it dulled the colors of her brilliant costume and made her seem like some unearthly creature of the night. He went down on knee, and she loomed over him, her plumed headdress making her even taller.

"Poppy—," he began, but she hissed and he stopped. He coughed, and tried to remember that this was part of a ruse and not a real proposal. "Ella, my love," he said, trying to sound infatuated. "Will you do me the very great honor of, um, making me, I mean, becoming my bride?"

"Oh, la! I am too flattered!" Poppy's voice was high-pitched, and Christian couldn't tell if she was mocking Eleanora or frightened. "But of course I accept!" She smacked his shoulder with her fan as though knighting him.

Suddenly, there was a crash like a thousand plates smashing to the floor at once, and Poppy reeled. Christian leaped to his feet and took hold of her waist to steady her. Within the palace, all the clocks began to chime.

"It can't be midnight," Poppy gasped. "It's only been a few minutes since eleven!"

"It's the Corley's doing!" Christian gripped her waist even harder as she started to pull away from him, her face contorted beneath the feathered mask. "What's wrong?"

"She's calling me . . . I have to go!"

Poppy slipped from his arms and ran, back into the ballroom, through the crowd of guests. No one was dancing, they were all milling about in confusion as the clocks continued to chime and chime.

As they tore through the front doors, Christian heard others following him. A quick look back showed Roger, Marianne, and the rest of their friends in pursuit. Outside, a golden carriage shaped like a round market basket was pulled up at the bottom of the steps, and the footmen were practically dancing in place with anxiety.

Poppy flew down the stairs, but tripped just as she reached the bottom. Christian reached out a hand, but one of the footmen all but threw her into the carriage. The coachman had the horses moving before she even sat down.

"Christian!" There was real terror in her voice as the carriage racketed away.

"This way!" Roger grabbed Christian before he tried to chase after Poppy on foot.

Another carriage had pulled up, and Christian saw Lord and Lady Seadown climbing into it, giving orders to the coachman to go straight to their manor at once.

"What's that?" Marianne had stopped just as Dickon was

trying to help her into the carriage. She was pointing at something near Christian's feet.

The prince looked down just in time to avoid stepping on a high-heeled shoe of exquisite blue and gold glass. He bent and scooped it up, then leaped onto the seat of the Seadowns' carriage beside the coachman.

Imposter

The golden carriage barreled through the rear gates of Seadown House and aimed straight for the banked bonfire Poppy could see waiting there in front of the stable. It was her last chance to quit, to jump to safety, but she just gripped the side of the carriage and said a quick prayer as they passed through the ashes and into the Corley's palace.

The carriage slid to a stop, the horses nearly falling to their rumps on the slick glass floor. All the servants leaped off of their perches and one of them grabbed Poppy's arm, hauling her out of the carriage like a sack of potatoes.

"Do you mind?" She clambered to her feet, straightening her elaborate skirts with great dignity.

What she saw next made her heartily glad for the man's rough manners, however.

Before their eyes the carriage was melting. In a matter of seconds it was nothing but a sizzling pile of orange gold slag in the middle of the floor. Poppy gulped, thinking what it would have been like to be trapped in the carriage as it melted.

She turned to thank the footman, but he, too, was gone. All the servants had faded back to wherever they came from, and so had the horses. At least, she thought they had. But there were twelve fat white rats scuttling around the smoldering remains of the carriage, their pink noses wiggling. One of them had a distinctly horsey look, Poppy thought, as it peered up at her. Then they all turned and scampered off to some unseen hole.

And Poppy was alone.

"Hello?"

She looked around. The room was circular, and there seemed to be one way in or out: an arch just large enough for her to pass through. The only sign of the carriage's entrance was a streak of greasy soot on the floor. She took a step toward the arch, and yelped with pain as something stabbed her instep.

Raising her skirts high, she looked down to find that the glass slipper on her left foot had broken in half. The glass, which had been uncomfortably hot but pliable during the ball, had hardened now. Her right shoe was missing entirely, and Poppy couldn't for the life of her remember where she had lost it.

She probed her feet with a wary finger, but there was no sign of the glassy hardness that had affected Eleanora. The broken glass had scratched her instep, but it was shallow and hardly bled. She knotted one of her abundant layers of underskirt into a pocket and slipped the two halves of the glass slipper inside.

Then Poppy padded off to find the Corley.

"Hello?" She called out with false bravado as she passed through half a dozen empty glass rooms. "He proposed . . . I accepted . . . I want to go now."

She turned a corner and found herself in the Corley's throne room. The old witch was crouched on her throne like a toad, eyes glittering, and her silent court gathered around, watching Poppy as she stumbled into the room.

"Well?" Poppy held out her arms, hoping that they didn't shake or her voice tremble. "Here I am. Prince Christian proposed. Can I go now? Um, to be with my prince?"

The Corley laughed.

"Do you think I am a fool?" she asked sweetly. "Christian was to propose to Lady Ella. But he didn't. He proposed to you, Princess *Poppy*. You should be sipping tea in the Seadown parlor while Ella dreams of her marriage. But instead you've ruined everything."

Poppy's blood froze in her veins.

"Like your dreams of getting your goddaughter back?" Poppy choked out. "Eleanora isn't Mary Bess, you know. Nothing can bring her back from the dead."

"Don't you say her name!" The Corley shook with rage, leaping from her throne and coming at Poppy with hands outstretched, her fingers like talons. "Don't ever say her name! She was mine! My goddaughter—my child! He stole her in the night, took her away to marry that spoiled prince!"

Poppy stepped back but the Corley didn't advance, just stood there in the middle of her throne room with her face

transfigured by madness and her hands clutching at something unseen.

"Now I have my Eleanora," she ranted. "I'll give her whatever she wants: gowns, jewels, a handsome husband, and she will never leave me!"

Poppy pulled the pistol out of her skirts and pointed it at the Corley. Her hands were shaking so badly, however, that she knew her shot would go wild. "Then let me go," she said, her voice hardly more than a whisper.

Poppy needed to get out, fast. Before the Corley decided to kill her for impersonating Eleanora. Or worse, wanted to keep her as a substitute goddaughter. She was so cold with terror that her cheeks felt frozen, and there was not a drop of moisture in her mouth. Even in the Palace Under Stone she had not felt this frightened, or in this much danger.

"You tried to trick me," the Corley said, her voice raw. "But I caught you." She wagged a gnarled finger at Poppy. "So now we're going to play a little game, to see which one of you he really loves. If he picks you, Eleanora will stay with me forever, and you can marry your handsome prince. And if he picks her . . ." The Corley's mouth stretched into a too-wide smile. "Why then I will have a new goddaughter to dote on."

The Corley clapped her hands, and two servants entered the room. Sagging between them, clad only in a nightgown and with her feet clinking against the glass floor, was Eleanora.

"Time to freshen up!" The Corley clapped her hands and more servants appeared. "Your prince will be here soon!"

Rescuer

Cursing, Christian saw the golden carriage disappear into the ashes, which swirled away before the Thwaite horses could reach them. They drove through the sooty mark on the cobblestones twice, just to make certain, but nothing happened.

The coachman finally halted the horses, and Roger helped the ladies disembark. Christian jumped down from his seat and ran into Seadown House. In the kitchen there was a roaring fire, and the maid tending it shrieked as he grabbed up a kettle of water and threw it on the flames. He coughed as the steam rose up in his face, grabbing a poker to stir the ashes and make sure no lick of fire still burned.

"Your lordship, your ladyship," the scullery maid said tearfully when her master and mistress entered. "I was waiting up to make you tea, but then *he* tossed the kettle on the fire," she finished, pointing an indignant finger at Christian.

"It's all right, my girl," Lord Richard said kindly. "We needed some wet ash for . . . removing our masks. Glued on, you know." He tapped the edge of his mask, which was quite noticeably tied on with a ribbon. "You run along to bed, and we'll take care of it ourselves."

The scullery maid clearly thought her master had gone mad, but was in no position to argue with him. So off to bed she went, with many fearful looks over her shoulder.

As soon as she was gone, Christian looked to the others to see if they were ready. Roger and Dickon drew their long knives, and Lord Richard nodded. Christian spoke the rhyme and waited, but nothing happened.

Roger came forward and tried it, and so did Marianne, Lady Margaret, and Dickon.

"She's shut us out," Christian said. "And Poppy is trapped there."

"I'll fetch Eleanora," Roger said. "It might work for her."

Roger came running back into the kitchen only a few minutes later, face white and sweat glistening on his forehead.

"She's gone."

They all gaped at him.

"Eleanora's gone, and there's soot all over the carpet in her bedroom."

"The Corley," Lady Margaret gasped.

"Now that she has them both, what will she do?" Marianne clung to her mother's waist, and Lady Margaret put an arm around her daughter.

Christian punched the rough stones of the fireplace, feeling a dark satisfaction as his knuckles sparked with pain and blood blossomed across the split skin.

"Let me try," Lord Richard said, his voice brittle.

"Sir, if you would," Christian said gratefully.

"I will not say it is my pleasure," Lord Richard said, with a ghost of his usual humor.

The elegant earl took out his handkerchief and spat into it. Then he laid the white square over the damp ashes in the hearth and knelt beside it.

"Corley, Mistress, Queen of Glass,
Open the doors that I may pass."

At once the broad hearth stretched itself up into an arching doorway. Lord Richard turned and raised one eyebrow at Christian.

"Your Highness?"

Christian didn't need to be asked twice. Short sword gripped tight, he strode through the ashes with his companions at his heels. The floor turned from sooty hearthstones to glass, and then the glass turned sticky, and they fell through a hole into nothing.

Double

The room filled with soot and cinders, startling Eleanora out of a doze. She had planned to stay awake all night, until Roger and Poppy and the others returned, but her feet were so heavy and she was so wrung out with emotion that she finally fell asleep.

And then *they* came, in the midst of the ashes, and snatched her out of bed. The Corley's servents were huge, but they burst from the fireplace as lightly as dancers, lifted her up, and returned to their mistress in the space of a heartbeat.

"Did you think that I wouldn't know?" The Corley tsk'd at her. "Did you think that that foreign princess could fool me?"

Eleanora felt weak. She couldn't walk, couldn't escape, couldn't think what to do next. They had had no real plan, only to replace Eleanora with Poppy and hope there was some chink in the Corley's glass armor. But there was none, and now Eleanora was in her godmother's palace and had no way of knowing if she would ever see Roger or the others again.

"I don't like it when my goddaughters disobey me," the Corley told her. "We shall have to see about your punishment."

"Godmother dear," Eleanora said in a timid voice. "I didn't mean to upset you. But my feet . . . I couldn't walk! Poppy was only trying to help." She bit her lip, not having to feign her uncertainty. "Could you . . . will you let us go now?"

The Corley gave her a disdainful look. "You betrayed me, and now you must pay the price. I have half a mind to let my spell run its course and turn the rest of you to glass. You would make a lovely addition to the statues in the throne room, you disobedient little baggage."

Eleanora fainted.

When she recovered, she was still being held up by the two servants, her hard glass feet slipping against the floor. Poppy was there, chalky pale and clearly trying to put on a brave front. They were taken down the hall to the dressing room where Eleanora had dreamed of marrying Prince Christian and spending her life dancing in palaces.

Surrounded by mute servants, with the Corley looking on with an expression of malicious glee, Eleanora was dressed in a gown of peacock silk and plumes exactly like Poppy's. Her hair was done in the same elaborate coiffure, cosmetics applied, and then a mask. Poppy's hair was tidied, her lip rouge freshened, and her mask tightened in place as well.

"I am so sick of being dressed like someone else," Eleanora said as the two of them stared at their twin reflections in the mirror.

Poppy gave a startled laugh.

"Don't worry," she said. "When this is all over and we've won, I'm sure that Roger will buy you dozens of gowns, all unique."

"When we've won?" Eleanora reached over and took Poppy's hand.

"Yes," the princess said firmly. "Sometime around dawn, I'm guessing."

"So confident, Your Highness," the Corley said. "You might make an excellent goddaughter as well. Perhaps I shall keep you both, no matter the outcome of my little contest."

"Contest?" The back of Eleanora's neck prickled.

"A little exercise, really, to see if our handsome yet spoiled prince can recognize his true love."

She snapped her fingers, and a servant brought a tray with two goblets. She gave one to each girl, and Eleanora exchanged an uneasy look with Poppy.

"What is it?" They asked at the same time.

"Just drink!" The Corley's voice was hard.

Poppy shrugged and raised her glass to Eleanora.

Eleanora tried to return the salute, but her hand was shaking and she nearly spilled her drink. She gulped it down quickly, praying that it wasn't poison, although that would hardly serve the Corley's purposes.

"Much better," the Corley beamed.

Poppy opened her mouth to reply, and frowned as her lips moved but no sound came out.

The Game

Christian didn't know where he was. In fact, for what seemed to be a very long time, he didn't know *who* he was. He was lying on a cold, slick surface, and his wrists itched. When he scratched at the rough woolen bands around his wrists he remembered that his name was Christian, and that he was a prince.

Sitting up, he also remembered that he was looking for someone. A princess. She was to be his bride and he had lost her somewhere here in this strange cold place. Where was she?

"Hello?"

He looked around. He was in a room made of green glass. It was round, and even the floor curved, rather like being in a bubble. There was an archway leading out of the bubble, and as he stepped toward it, something fell from his pocket and landed on the floor with a chime.

Looking down, Christian found a woman's high-heeled dancing slipper, made of exquisitely blown glass in blue and green and gold. He picked it up, and a brief flash of memory told him that it belonged to his love, who had lost it entering her golden carriage. He was bringing it to her now, and he held it tightly to keep from dropping it again.

"Hello?"

He carried the slipper out of the green room, into a red room, then an orange. Was there nothing more here but a long silent chain of round glass rooms? He saw no other signs of life, heard no sounds but that of his footsteps and his breath.

Gazing around a pale rose room, he thought he saw something glimmering through one of the walls. Stepping closer, he could just make out a figure through the glass. Not his own reflection, but what appeared to be a woman. She knocked on the glass, frantic, as though trying to reach him.

"Step back, step back," he shouted to her. His heart racing—it was his bride-to-be, he knew it—Christian raised his foot and began to kick the wall. He wished he were wearing boots and riding breeches instead of oddly shaped velvet slippers and cumbersome robes, but he couldn't remember why he was dressed this way, either.

At last the wall splintered, and he helped the young woman step through. She was clad in billowing trousers and a tight, low-cut bodice, and he made a note to ask her to dress more modestly once they were wed.

"Is it you?" He studied her face, now feeling doubtful. She did have dark hair, and the fuzzy image in his mind of his bride was also dark haired. He held up the slipper. "Is this yours? Are you her?"

They both looked at her feet. They were bare, and the

reflected glow of the pink floor made them look pearly and perfect.

Christian knelt and offered her the slipper. She slid her foot into it and stepped down. Her dark brows were knit with concentration.

"It might be mine," she said, and took a step.

The shoe slipped off her foot and she stumbled, catching herself on the slick, curving wall.

"I don't think so," Christian said. "I shall keep looking."

"May I join you?" Her lower lip trembled. "I think I'm looking for someone, too, and I don't want to be alone."

"Of course." Christian picked up the slipper, took her arm with his free hand, and together they walked out of the pink room into a blue one.

Through the wall of this room they spied a number of other people, and Christian and the men on the other side managed to break a large hole in the wall so that the three strangers could cross through. They were a stately older couple and a young man with a bare chest. Christian tried the slipper on the lady, even though she seemed too old to be his bride. Her narrow foot was too long for the slipper, so they all shrugged and moved forward.

The young man took the arm of the girl in the billowing trousers, and she smiled shyly up at him in a way that made Christian jealous. The girl said her name was Marianne, and she seemed relatively certain that this Dickon was the person she was looking for, but in this strange glass world there was no way to be completely sure.

They passed through more rooms, until they met another young man, this one bearing a strong resemblance to Dickon. He said his name was Roger. Roger, too, was looking for a dark-haired girl who was to be his bride, which made Dickon draw Marianne all the closer. But Roger peered into her face and shook his head.

"Someone else, someone else," he muttered.

"I, too," Christian said, brandishing the slipper. "Come with us."

They came to a room of gold, and Christian knew they were at the end.

In the middle of the room sat two young women in small golden glass chairs. Both were dressed alike in peacock blue ball gowns, festooned with real peacock plumes, and both wore feathered masks and had dark hair.

"Which one of you is my bride?" Christian studied them both, his pulse racing. She was here . . . one of these beautiful girls . . . but which one?

Neither of them spoke, though one lifted a hand and then dropped it, looking over her shoulder at the shadows behind her.

"May I try this slipper on you both? It belongs to my bride," Christian said, not sure what else to do.

"By all means," said a kind voice. The shadows stirred and a plump woman in a lace cap and shawl came forward. Her grandmotherly demeanor made Christian smile. The old woman laughed like tinkling glass. "Try the slipper on both of our young ladies, if you please! It will fit only your true love!"

His true love! At last, he would find her! Sinking to his knees, Christian held out the slipper to the girl on the left. She lifted her feathery skirts and presented her bare foot.

Christian started to slide the glass dancing slipper over her toes, but then he hesitated. There was something wrong with her feet. They shone in the dim light like hard, milky glass. He looked up into her eyes, a question on his lips.

Her eyes were blue.

That wasn't right, either.

He looked at the next young woman, on his right. She raised her skirts to offer her foot. It was smooth and pale, too, but skin and not glass. Clutching the slipper so tightly that the filigreed design was leaving deep ridges in his palms, he gazed into her eyes, and saw that they were a beautiful deep violet. He realized that the wool bracelets around his wrists had stopped itching at last.

A sigh escaped Christian, and he put the slipper on his true love's foot.

The corner of her mouth quirked up in a wry smile, and she pulled two pieces of broken glass from a fold of her gown. She bent down and fitted the broken pieces to her foot like a jigsaw puzzle.

"Thank you," she said to Christian. "It's so vexing to lose a single shoe."

"Poppy?" The name came to his lips easily.

She laughed and threw her arms around his neck. "It took you long enough," she said, and planted a kiss on his lips.

"Roger?" The other girl stretched out her arms to the tall young man, tried to stand, and fell.

Roger rushed to gather her in his arms.

"No! No!"

The Corley—Christian's memories were as clear as glass now—began to scream and stamp her feet. The walls around them began to glow brighter, and Christian drew Poppy in close.

"No! No!"

The old witch seemed to swell and her face was dark purple. She gestured with clawed fingers and servants came running with strange tools and pans of molten glass.

He felt a tug on his arm, and found Marianne there.

"Let's go," she whispered. Her other arm was linked in Poppy's, and she was drawing them both toward the door.

Lady Margaret was beckoning to them silently from the passageway. Lord Richard was helping Roger with Eleanora.

"Where is the Corley?" Marianne's eyes were wide and her voice sounded strangled. Her grip on Christian's arm loosened and she grabbed at Dickon. "She was right here . . ."

"Run, now!" Lord Richard's voice was low and urgent.

However the Corley traveled through the walls of her palatial glass prison, it was by no means that Christian could detect. They ran down a passageway and found themselves in a round green room that had no other door he could see.

They turned to go back, and the Corley was there, a seething pot of molten glass in her hands.

"This is my realm," she hissed. "And if I wish to keep you here forever, I will!"

The Corley spilled the pot of molten glass at their feet. The floor began to bubble and melt.

"Keep clear!" Christian wrapped an arm around Poppy, who was closest to the Corley.

"I am not staying here," Poppy shouted, shaking him off.

She turned to the nearest wall and shot it point blank with her pistol. Then she leaped through the shattered ruin, pulling Christian with her. They found themselves in another round room, and Poppy used the butt of her pistol to break the far wall.

Christian joined her, smashing at the walls with the hilt of his long knife. Together they moved on and on through an endless chain of glass rooms until suddenly, screaming, Poppy smashed through a wall of sapphire glass and they found themselves tumbling onto the hearth rug of the Seadowns' parlor. Someone snatched Poppy by the shoulders, and Christian cried out and reached for her as she thrashed and cursed.

"Poppy! Stop that! It's me, Rose!"

And Poppy collapsed into her sister's arms and burst into tears.

Betrothed

Poppy was mortally embarrassed to be crying in front of everyone, but they were free of the Corley and Rose and Galen had come and she just couldn't stop herself. She threw her arms around her oldest sister and blubbered like a three-year-old until Rose finally sat her on a sofa and told her sternly to calm down.

"It's over, isn't it?" Poppy asked, hiccupping.

"Of course it is," Rose soothed her.

"I suppose some explanations all around might be in order," Lord Richard said.

"And tea," said Lady Margaret. She gave the bell-pull a firm yank.

A maid put her head into the room immediately, her face all curiosity. "Ma'am?"

"Tea, sandwiches, cakes, whatever Cook can provide," Lady Margaret said.

"Perhaps we should start with introductions," Lord Richard said, smiling slightly despite the severe look in his eyes.

Poppy rallied and introduced Rose and Galen, since she was the only person in the room who knew who they were. This caused a great deal of excitement, and a lot of hugging, as Lady Margaret and Marianne immediately threw themselves at Rose, whom they knew only through letters, while Galen shook hands all around and gave Poppy a rib-cracking hug.

Then she told her side of what had happened, feeling quite limp by the end of the narrative.

By the time she was done, Marianne and Eleanora were in tears and the maids had brought in the trays and been dismissed. Christian set a plate of sandwiches and cakes in Poppy's lap and insisted with great concern that she eat.

"I will if you will," she said, and he sat at her feet and helped himself to his own plateful.

Rose raised her eyebrows at this, but Poppy refused to be baited. Not right now, at least.

"We got your letter, Poppy," Galen said.

"Which one?"

His strong-jawed face cracked with amusement. "The first one, I suppose. And we immediately sent to Walter for advice. He didn't like the sound of it, either, not the dreams nor any of your uneasy feelings.

"We wrote to Prince Christian as well," Galen said, frowning. "Trying to warn him, because we knew if it was the Corley, she might set her sights on another Dane prince. But we never got an answer."

Christian turned bright red, and muttered something about Lady Ella, and feeling like a fool.

Galen gave him a coolly appraising look and then looked to Poppy. She felt herself blushing, and raised her chin.

"My feet!" Eleanora sat bolt upright and raised her skirts to her knees. "My feet!"

Poppy's heart lurched, and she wondered if the other girl's glass feet had cracked or something equally horrible. Then she saw that Eleanora was beaming and wiggling her toes.

"They're healed," she sobbed. "Does this mean—am I—are we all free of the Corley?" With one hand she stroked at her feet, and with the other she clutched at Roger as though she were drowning.

Poppy felt a pang of jealousy at the raw emotion on Roger's normally reserved face. Then she felt the weight of Christian's head on her own knee, and stroked his hair.

"Yes," Galen said. "You are free of the Corley. All the bargains that have been made with her are now void. Walter and I will consult with some of the Bretoner mages to do what we can to seal her in her realm forever."

"Which means, my dear, that no one can stop me from providing you with a home," Lord Richard said to Eleanora. He, too, took in her continued close proximity to Roger. "And though it will do little to repair the damage I did to your family, Eleanora, I would be more than pleased to present you with a dowry."

"What about Marianne's dowry?" Dickon Thwaite took Marianne's hand in his.

Lord Richard looked him up and down. "After the overly familiar way you have been behaving with my daughter, especially since she donned that *highly inappropriate* costume this evening, I expect you to propose even if her dowry is an old shoe!"

"Yes sir," Dickon said sheepishly.

"Who do I speak to about Poppy?" Christian looked from Lord Richard to Galen and then to Rose.

Poppy left off stroking his hair. "Who do you speak to about what?" She wasn't sure why her voice came out quite so sharp, but she didn't bother to apologize.

Laughing, Rose pinched Poppy's arm.

"Ouch! Rose, stop that!"

"I'm quite anxious for the rest of your letters to catch up to us," Rose said slyly. "But in the meantime, Prince Christian, we should probably send a letter to our fathers. Kings like to be involved in this sort of thing."

"What sort of thing?" Again, Poppy's voice came out shrill. Were they really talking about . . . ? She was only sixteen! But Christian . . . Well, he had picked her over Eleanora, even under the Corley's enchantment.

"We are the future rulers of Westfalin," Galen said to Rose, clearly enjoying Poppy's confusion. "We could make some of the arrangements ourselves, Rosie."

"I'd actually like the chance to plan a more romantic setting for the proposal," Christian said.

"Yes! No!" Poppy knew her face was so red it was probably glowing.

"No?" Christian twisted around and climbed up on his knees to look at her. "You mean you don't want to?"

"I'm only sixteen . . . we hardly know each other!"

Christian's face clouded, and Poppy felt her heart plummet toward her feet.

"You could always ask me. I mean . . ."

His expression cleared. "Princess Poppy, would you care to visit the Danelaw for the holidays?"

"Yes! I do! I will!" Poppy hugged him and then leaped back, embarrassed. "You could propose to me later, in a more private setting," she said. "Just to see if things change," she told him. "Besides, I need to let my feet rest. Betrothals and weddings always involve a great deal of dancing."

The rest of the room looked on in shock.

"Dancing? You, Poppy?" Marianne shook her head slowly. "I never thought . . ."

Rose looked concerned. She even felt Poppy's forehead for fever, but Poppy shook her off.

"I don't know about you, Rose, but I am done with letting creatures like Under Stone or the Corley dictate my life. I enjoy dancing, and I will blasted well dance at my wedding!"

"Poppy! Language!"

Poppy didn't answer; she just threw her arms around Christian and kissed him soundly.

The Anti-Love-Spell Bracelet

Materials:

1 skein worsted weight yarn

Size 7 (US) straight knitting needles

1 cable needle (abbreviation: CN)

Blunt yarn needle

1 button (shanked)

Instructions:

Cast on six stitches.

Row 1: K1, M1 by knitting through the front and back of the stitch, K2, M1, K1 (8 stitches)

Row 2: Knit

Row 3: K1, M1, K4, M1, K1 (10 stitches)

Row 4: Knit

Begin charm pattern. Charm is based on the Hugs & Kisses cable.

Row 1: P1, K8, P1

Row 2: K1, P8, K1

Row 3: P1, slip 2 stitches to CN and hold to back of work, K2, K2 from CN, slip 2 stitches to CN, hold to front of work, K2, K2 from CN, P1.

Row 4: K1, P8, K1

Row 5: P1, K8, P1

Row 6: K1, P8, K1

Row 7: repeat Row 3
Row 8: K1, P8, K1
Row 9: P1, K8, P1
Row 10: K1, P8, K1
Row 11: P1, slip 2 stitches to CN and hold to FRONT of work, K2, K2 from CN, slip 2 stitches to CN, hold to BACK of work, K2, K2 from CN, P1.
Row 12: K1, P8, K1
Row 13: P1, K8, P1
Row 14: K1, P8, K1
Row 15: repeat Row 11
Row 16: K1, P8, K1
Knit these 16 rows 3 times, or to desired length.

Finish:
Row 1: Knit
Row 2: Purl
Row 3: Knit
Row 4: Knit
Row 5: K1, K2tog, K4, K2tog, K1
Row 6: Knit
Row 7: K1, K2tog, cast off 2 stitches, K2tog, K1
Row 8: K3, cast on 1, K3. (This creates a buttonhole.)
Row 9: K1, K2tog, K1, K2tog, K1
Row 10: K all stitches together, pull yarn through loop and tie off.
Weave in ends. Center and sew button to beginning half inch of bracelet, use buttonhole created at the end to fasten.

The Poppy Flower Stole

Materials:

200 yds. sport weight yarn

Size 10 (US) knitting needles (circular will give you more room)

Blunt yarn needle for finishing

Instructions:

In order to form a border of poppy flowers on each end of the stole, you will knit two 2½ foot pieces and graft them together using the Kitchener stitch, explained below.

Cast on 100 stitches.

Row 1: Knit 3, purl 4, K1, P4, K1, P4, K1, P4, K3. Repeat three more times, to end of row.

Row 2, and all even numbered rows: Knit the knit stitches and purl the purls.

Row 3: K2, yarn over (YO), K1 P2, P2 together, K1, P4, K1, P4, K1, P2tog, P2, K1, YO, K2. Repeat.

Row 5: K3, YO, K1, P3, K1, P2, P2tog, K1, P2tog, P2, K1, P3, K1, YO, K3. Repeat.

Row 7: K4, YO, K1, P1, P2tog, K1, P3, K1, P3, K1, P2tog, P1, K1, YO, K4. Repeat.

Row 9: K5, YO, K1, P2, K1, P1, P2tog, K1, P2tog, P1, K1, P2, K1, YO, K5. Repeat.

Row 11: K6, YO, K1, P2tog, K1, P2, K1, P2, K1, P2tog, K1, YO, K6. Repeat.
Row 13: K7, YO, K1, P1, K1, P2tog, K1, P2tog, K1, P1, K1, YO, K7. Repeat.
Row 15: K1, YO, K7, YO, K2tog, K2tog, K2tog, K2tog, K1, YO, K7, YO, K1. Repeat.
Row 16: as previous even numbered rows.
These 16 rows form the poppy border of the stole. The "stems" form the body of the stole, and consist of a two row pattern.

Row 1: slip the first stitch, K11, P1, K12, repeat to end.
Row 2: slip the first stitch, P11, K1, P12, repeat to end.
Work these two rows until piece measures 2½ feet, or half the desired length of the stole. Slip piece, without casting off and being careful not to drop any stitches, onto a piece of scrap yarn and set aside. Make a second piece, beginning again with the poppy border and stems.

Grafting: slide first piece back onto a needle, and hold both pieces together with the purl sides facing each other. Thread the yarn through a yarn needle, and insert the needle through the first stitch of the front knitting needle as if to knit. Drawing the yarn through the stitch, slip the stitch off the needle. Insert the yarn needle through the second stitch of the front needle as if to purl, draw yarn through, but don't drop the stitch yet. Now insert the yarn needle through the first stitch of the back needle as if to purl, draw yarn through, and slip stitch off. Insert the yarn needle through the second stitch of the back needle as if to knit, draw the yarn through, and leave the stitch on the needle.

Repeat until all stitches have been grafted and dropped off, weave in yarn ends.

Acknowledgments

I always imagined writing a book to be a solitary exercise, envisioning myself toiling away in a garret, alone, like Louisa May Alcott.

And then I actually wrote a book, and discovered that it takes a village to raise a novel. Which is why many thanks must go out to all my nearest and dearest for this book as well.

First off, my husband. You must have a special kind of madness to write a book, and a special kind of patience to marry a writer. My husband cooks, cleans, watches the children, and listens to my rants with amazing patience and love, and I thank him.

Secondly, my family, both biological and in-law, who are supportive to the extreme. Their continued cheerleading, not to mention free babysitting, makes it not only worthwhile but possible.

Then there's my amazing agent, Amy Jameson. Despite having her own little ones underfoot, she somehow still manages to keep track of me and my projects, give me great feedback, and yes, listen to me rant.

Melanie Cecka and all the great people at Bloomsbury are an author's dream. I couldn't ask for a better editor to help me fine-tune my books, or a more stellar team for putting the "pretty" on my books and getting them into the hands of the reader!

Special thanks to my children, also. My son, at the tender age of five, is not only proud of his mommy but also understands what "Mommy needs to write!" means. My daughter is frankly no help at all, but she is adorable and wonderful in every way, and so this book is hers.

Jessica Day George

is the author of five previous novels, including *Princess of the Midnight Ball; Sun and Moon, Ice and Snow; Dragon Slippers; Dragon Flight;* and *Dragon Spear*. Originally from Idaho, she now lives in Salt Lake City, Utah, with her husband and two young children. She is currently working on *Tuesdays at the Castle,* a new novel about a magical castle that can build itself.

www.JessicaDayGeorge.com